# STEPS TO COURAGE

## By

## Sandra Stiles

Book design copyright © 2011 Karen Slimick Arnpriester. All
rights reserved.
Cover design by Karen Slimick Arnpriester
Interior design by Marlayne Jan Giron

Published in the United States of America by:

7290 B. Investment Drive
Charleston, SC 29418
USA
www.createspace.com

ISBN-13: 978-1460990285 (CreateSpace-Assigned)
ISBN-10: 1460990285
BISAC: General Fiction

# Dedication

Thank you to the wonderful students and teachers, Jesse, Cheyenne, and Emily, and Carol, who encouraged me to write books for my shelves, and read my manuscript along the way.

A special thank you to my nephew Chris Hackathorn, for information on life in the military, and Afghanistan. Thank you for serving to protect us.

Marlayne and Karen without your help with formatting and the book cover I would still be working on this book.

To my wonderful Agent Mary Jackson who made my dream come true, I look forward to many years with you.

I want to thank my husband who pushed me out of my comfort zone to make this book a reality, and listened to me as I read and re-read passages night after night. For believing in my ability and me when I often did not, know that I love you even more.

Most importantly, I want to thank God for blessing me with the desire to write.

Table of Contents

# 1 The Beginning

Mohamed could see the tower in front of him. He pointed the plane in its direction. Briefly, he thought back to the start of his morning. He had started his day with a prayer, and then headed to the Boston airport. Although he saw his friends in the terminal, he ignored them. Speaking to them might arouse suspicion and he needed to avoid raising suspicion at all cost. When they had announced his flight he boarded as if this was something he did every day. No one boarding with him would have suspected this would be his or her last flight. Mohamed took his seat next to his friend and colleague Abdulaziz. They greeted each other. Once the plane had lifted off, Mohamed took out the folder containing their plans. With their heads together, Mohamed and Abdulaziz looked like two ordinary business men discussing plans for a meeting. No one around them paid any attention to them. They had trained a long time for this day. They had moved from one state to another, training at different airports to keep suspicion down.

Mohamed looked at his watch. The timing had to be perfect if their plans were going to work. He gave the signal, and his partners on the plane quickly jumped up. Two of them took out the flight attendants in first class and a passenger sitting behind them. This commotion was enough to get the pilots to open the cockpit door. It was only a matter of minutes before they had total control of the plane.

The men quickly moved the passengers to the back of the plane. Mohamed tried to use the intercom to calm the passengers. With the flip of a switch, he told passengers they were returning to the airport and they should not be alarmed. He told them not to try anything because they had several planes in the air with bombs on board. Mohamed became alarmed when

1

the control tower asked him to repeat his last message. He had made his first mistake. He had not let the passengers know what was going on. With the flip of the wrong switch, he had just announced to the control tower, that there were several hijacked planes in the air. He did not care. It was too late to turn back now. "Allah's Will", would be done. This is why he had come to America, what he had trained for, and he was ready to die. He thought nothing about the innocent people in the Towers or on the plane. He had no idea that he would affect the lives of so many, including three teens on a mission of their own.

# 2  Trina

September eleventh began like any other day. There was no hint of the evil about to unfold. September days in New York usually began with a slight chill in the air, a hint that the lazy days of summer were over and the beginning of fall had arrived. The leaves had not yet started to turn colors; usually a sure sign that fall was on its way. Eighteen-year-old Trina Lacy waited for the turning of the leaves where the trees seemed to be in full bloom after changing colors. She loved this time of year. The turning leaves left a special smell in the air. The crisp air had a freshness that revitalized everything it touched, including her spirit.

Feeling the warm breeze blowing through her window, Trina's thoughts drifted to her busy day. She slowly drew back the sheet, stood up and stretched, feeling the pull of tight skin on her legs. The tight skin was no longer painful, just a daily reminder of the burns she had received a few years before. Excited about the day's events, Trina shuddered as an uneasy feeling washed over her. She pushed it aside believing it to be nothing more than a queasiness she often felt when her mind wandered to her accident. She quickly made her bed, then opened her closet and selected the outfit she would wear to school. She walked to the bathroom and prepared to step into the shower, trying unsuccessfully to avoid the full-length mirror. One glimpse brought back the memory of her accident. She had been sixteen at the time and the only things on her mind had been her looks, her boyfriend, and being the captain of the cheerleading squad. All of that ended on that horrible night. It had been almost two years since the accident and a day never went by that she did not think about it. Memories of that night could be sparked by something as trivial as hearing tires squeal on wet pavement, or watching someone get into their car and drive away from a bar. Her recovery had consisted of tortured days of endless pain that nearly consumed her. Days turned into weeks, and weeks into months of surgeries, skin grafts and rehabilitation. She had lived an eternal nightmare. The memory of the burns she sustained was still fresh even though most of the scars on her legs were gone or only slightly visible. Most of the scars she carried now were psychological, not physical. Trina winced once again, as these painful memories flooded her mind. She would give anything to have them completely disappear. Quickly she stepped into the shower to try to wash the haunting thoughts away. It was as if she was trying to put out a fire in her mind. She grabbed her lavender scented shampoo and body wash. The creamy feel of the soap made her feel refreshed and alive, while the slight scent of lavender relaxed her. On a busy day like today, she needed to relax. Feeling alive was something Trina would never again take for granted. She realized being alive was not just a physical experience but an experience for the mind and soul as well. She and her family had always gone to church. She even thought she had a good relationship with God until the accident. To get her through the endless days of pain after her accident, she relied on her faith.

It was then she began to think about life and what it really meant to be alive. Had she really been living? As a teenager, the number of parties you attended or the boy you dated was the measurement used to determine if you were living life to the fullest. Even your grades and your parents' response to those grades were a measurement of your life. She had plenty of time to re-evaluate her life, beliefs, and all that she held close to her heart while she lay in the hospital. She cried out to God when the pain was too much. She cried out in anger when she felt alone. Through it all, she wondered how people with no faith survived. She had to believe that there was a purpose to all of this. Was it to lead her back to God? Was it to give her the strength to move forward in life? She did not know but she understood that as long as she leaned on God she would, and could endure it all. She would survive. She would handle whatever was thrown her way. If there was one thing she had learned, it was that she could not do anything on her own.

Trina shook these thoughts from her mind as she stepped out of the shower. The soft towel felt comforting to the still tender tissue of her lower body. She dried off and began to dress in the outfit she had laid out. Unlike many of the students at Eagle Prep, she actually did not mind the school uniform. It took the guesswork out of what to wear each day. The school uniform consisted of a blue blazer with an eagle monogram, her choice of colored blouses, and a pair of navy pants or a skirt. She felt very grown up, and professional looking in her uniform, even if she was still in high school. She smiled as she remembered that just a few years before she had not cared how professional she looked. She just wanted to make sure she looked cute.

Trina had started out in a public school. Her grades had always been top of the list. She had always made honor roll and been up for one award after another. This did not seem to matter to her parents as she approached high school. Her parents were disappointed with the public education system. They began to look around at the different private schools. Through a co-worker, Trina's mother had learned about Eagle Prep. They scheduled a tour and an interview. They left the school pleased with what they had seen and impressed with its philosophy. The school believed in empowering students to meet everyday challenges. Personal and social development, academics and helping students find the self-worth they needed to survive in life accomplished this goal. The school believed in giving back to the community in many ways. It was not only a part of their curricular requirements, it was to become a part of their personal lives.

Once again, her mind wandered to her accident. She had never really thought about her school's philosophy, and how it applied to her life until she woke up in the hospital and realized the challenges that she would have to face because of her injuries. Lying in her hospital bed, she felt sorry for herself. It seemed so unfair. She allowed herself only a couple of days of this attitude. She decided she would not be a victim of her circumstances, she would survive them and then move on. Her body was burned, from just above her waist all the way down to her ankles. She knew she had months of surgery ahead of her. The first thing she had to do was come to grips with the withered and discolored skin. She sat while the nurses scraped the dead skin away. She looked at the fresh pink flesh underneath and reminded herself that things would be okay. Like the new skin under the dead, she would come out a new person. It helped that she was heavily medicated. Her mother had kept a recorder by her bedside at Trina's request. She wanted to record her thoughts so that later she could write them down. She needed a road map for her new life. The record of her time in the hospital would help her. She would build that new life from the pain of the old one. She wanted to look back at where she had come from. She told herself daily that her outer beauty was not all that she was. She had enough self-worth to know that she was and always had been beautiful inside. Convincing her mind to believe what her head knew was something else. This was her biggest uphill battle. Trina felt the breeze on her skin and once again brushed the cobweb of memories from her mind while she continued dressing.

She brought her thoughts back to her outfit and all of the walking she would have to do this day. She decided to wear the pants instead of the skirt, and a pair of sensible, slip on flats to round out her uniform. She seldom wore the skirt because of her scars. According to her parents and friends, they were barely visible anymore, but she still knew that they were there. It was amazing what a plastic surgeon could do these days. Too bad they did not have plastic surgery for the mind. She checked her reflection in the mirror, and was pleased to see, a well-groomed young woman reflected back. Everything was in its place. She pulled her strawberry blond hair neatly back at the nape of her neck with a barrette, giving her a business-like look. Her makeup was subtle yet brought out her bright green eyes. She applied the tiniest bit of lipstick to her thin lips to polish off the professional look she was going for. If she was going to be dealing with professionals, trying to persuade them to participate in her charity fund raiser, it was important that she look, act and speak professionally.

As a senior, Trina was well on her way to completing her required twenty-five hours of community service. All students at Eagle Prep were required to complete community service hours. In the elementary and middle grades, the school and parent groups set up the community service events. These included bake sales, spaghetti dinners, and making and delivering bagged lunches to the homeless shelters. High school students chose how they would earn those community hours from a list. The school required grades nine through twelve to complete twenty-five hours a year for graduation. Occasionally a student would come up with an idea and have to run it by the dean of the school. The dean would look over the proposal and decide whether to let the student proceed with it. Trina had come up with the idea of a charity fundraiser and the dean had been so impressed he had approved it immediately. He recognized the growth of a caring and giving spirit. At one time, he saw her as a bubbly cheerleader who thought only of herself and her boyfriend. The changes she had made to her own life and to the school were admirable. Since her accident, she was the first to volunteer for those less than desirable jobs. She always had a smile on her face. She was able to pull the most reluctant people to her side to help her with any project. He knew that what she had gone through after her accident had been terrible. Most adults would have given up or withdrawn into themselves. She had done just the opposite. She had spent her freshman through junior years working with the Red Cross, in one project after another. After the accident, her involvement in these projects increased. This time, she was in charge of a fundraiser to be held at Windows on the World. She and two other students were to meet at the World Trade Centers to finalize all of the details, and meet with a few other potential donors. She was so excited about this project because she was selected to lead it. She herself had come up with the idea. She had researched several worthy charities and decided to set up a fundraiser for something that meant so much to her.

This fundraiser would benefit all burn victims through the charity, "Angel Hope." Angel Hope truly cared about people. Angel Hope worked with people of all ages who had suffered a tragic injury. They were there to sit with patients through painful therapy or to play a game with the smallest patient. They offered a smile and friendship that many would find nowhere else. While recovering from her burns, volunteers from that organization had spent hours with her, helping her understand who she was. Identity was something that most burn victims lost in a fire or any severe burn incident. Most people would expect these volunteers to be adults. The volunteers who helped her were teens just like her that came and worked with other young children and teens. They let them know that they could see beyond the injury to the person inside. They made her feel safe and secure around others. This was something she had been afraid she would never feel.

After her accident, most of her friends had abandoned her. Her best friend Tracy had come to visit as soon as they allowed her to have visitors. When the biggest danger of infection was over, Tracy's mother brought her to see Trina. She had come like clockwork every afternoon at three, until the day she had walked in on Trina having her bandages changed.

"Hey Trina, do you want me to come back later?" She could see the pain in Trina's eyes.

Trina looked at her with glazed eyes that showed just how painful the procedure was. "No come in and sit by me. They've finished the legs and now we're up to the tummy. It's the most tender part and I could sure use a distraction right now."

Tracy walked to the bed. She took one look at the red and wrinkled skin on Trina's stomach and turned away. Trina saw the look of revulsion on Tracy's face.

"So what's happening at school?" Trina asked, trying to draw Tracy back to her.

"Not much. Suzie was made head cheerleader. I hope that doesn't bother you. She was your co-captain. I asked to be made co-captain under Suzie and they gave it to Janice." That's okay though."

Trina listened to her ramble on. "I think it's great that Suzie's the new captain. Tell her and Janice that I said congrats and that I miss all of them. Tell them if they can't get away from practice or anything that they can at least call me."

"Sure, I'll tell them. Listen, I've got to go. We're going over to Suzie's house to practice and I'll give them the message."

Tracy turned and almost ran from the room. She did not even give Trina time to say goodbye. That was the last she had seen of Tracy. Tracy had called a couple of times after that and then even the phone calls stopped. At first, Trina was sad and hurt. Then she felt angry. She knew her friends were not trying to be cruel. They did not know what to say or where to look when they were around her. She understood this, but it did not make the hurt and anger she felt go away. Just because her body made them uncomfortable was no reason to desert her. That is what they had done. They had deserted her in her hour of need. It made her look at her relationship with her friends. Was she this shallow as a friend to others? When she thought back about the way she had often treated others because the situation made her uncomfortable, then she realized she had been as guilty as they had.

Some of the volunteers from Angel Hope, like Alyssa, were burn victims themselves. At the age of three Alyssa had pulled a pan of boiling water off the stove. She had suffered second and third degree burns over eighty percent of her body. It was a miracle that she had survived the burns. When Alyssa had first walked into the room, Trina had prayed that she would not remain as scarred as Alyssa. Immediately she felt horrified that she had felt so repulsed by this girl's appearance. This girl was there to give her hope and she was not going to let the negativity or fear get the best of her. After getting to know Alyssa, she thought back on that first meeting day and felt ashamed. She had not realized at that time, that Alyssa still had more surgeries to go through that would help to change her appearance and eliminate most of the remaining scars. Because Alyssa was so young when her accident happened, and she was still growing, she had to have her procedures done in smaller steps to accommodate that growth. Now that she was almost fifteen she would soon be getting the final surgeries that would change her appearance. Trina still struggled with understanding that what she looked like on the outside did not make her the person she was on the inside.

These sudden memories made Trina apprehensive about Mark and Lucas, her two partners in this fundraiser. She did not know much about Mark except he was the quiet type. He had very few friends at school that she knew of. Of course, she really had not gone out of her way to get to know him. She had friends but she was not into the gossip the way she had been at one time. She hung with everyone and no one. Her closest friends were those she had met through Angel Hope.

All that Trina knew about Mark was that he had entered Eagle Prep the previous school year in March. Because he seemed to be such a loner, she was shocked when he had volunteered for this assignment. She had heard that something tragic had happened to his family involving a fire. Maybe that tragic connection had made him volunteer. She had never asked anyone for details about him or his family because she knew what it was like when people asked questions that made you feel uncomfortable. She hoped that she would be able to get to know him better during the time they worked together on the fundraiser. Maybe she would find out why this community service project seemed so important to him. He had almost knocked his chair over to volunteer for it. She was pleased to see him step up to the plate. Maybe they could become friends.

Besides, he was one of the better-looking people at school and it was time she got back into the dating game.

The other member of her team was Lucas, her former boyfriend. They had not really spoken to each other since the accident. She had mixed feelings about having him on the team. A part of her still cared for him and was thrilled that he had volunteered. She was afraid of his reasons for volunteering. Was it out of pity, or guilt? She hoped it was for none of those. She would welcome him to the project. However, she could never forget the hurtful words she had overheard him say while she was lying in the hospital. She thought she had forgiven and forgotten until he volunteered to be on their team. Memories of the good times they had had came flooding back. The only thing she could hope for was that he would be civil to her and that she could keep old feelings of anger from resurfacing. Everyone knew her reasons for suggesting this project. They knew it was her personal connections with Angel Hope that meant so much to her, and the last thing she needed from Lucas was pity. If there was only one thing she had learned during recovery, it was not to judge people, so she would give Lucas a chance and hope that things worked out for the best.

Trina walked down the steps from her bedroom to the second floor kitchen. She like the way her house was laid out. She had the third floor all to herself. She had her bedroom and bathroom as well as a sitting room just off the bedroom. She spent a lot of time there reading. The windows faced the water so she could spend relaxing days while recovering.

As she walked into the kitchen she saw her mother was frantically searching her purse trying to find her keys. Trina saw the empty cups next to the coffee maker, poured them both a cup of coffee, and headed out to the deck. She loved eating breakfast, or just drinking her coffee out here where she could hear the sounds of the birds chirping in the morning sunshine. She loved her home. The only place she loved more was their cottage on the beach, where she had done most of her recuperating. With an exasperated huff, her mother came out onto the deck and plopped down in a chair.

Trina looked at her mother quizzically, "Okay, what has you so frazzled?"

"I received a call from work and my secretary informed me I have an eight-thirty meeting. I wouldn't be so concerned except I've had trouble getting things together this morning, including myself. I hate to rush you, but we have to leave in about ten minutes so we can catch the ferry."

Trina chuckled at her mother's look of exasperation. It was so unlike her mother to be frazzled. In the worst situation she was the one who held it all together. She hoped one day to figure out how to obtain just a little bit of the strength and togetherness her mother possessed. They quickly finished their coffee and Trina took their coffee cups back into the kitchen. She rushed back upstairs to brush her teeth while her mother pulled the car out of the garage. Trina grabbed her purse from the hall table and rushed down the stairs. As she stepped out of the front door of the house, she stopped. She had the strangest feeling she would never see her house again. Shaking the silly idea from her mind, she ran to the car and got in. She fastened her seatbelt and once again had the nagging feeling that she should just stay home. She looked over at her mother, smiled and said, "Let's go." For some reason she just could not shake the uneasy feeling that had plagued her all morning.

Trina and her mother started the drive to the ferry in silence. A million questions were going through her mother's mind and she was not sure if she should ask any of them. If she wanted them answered she figured she would just have to risk it, and asked the first question.

"So, how long do you think you'll be at the Trade Center?"

"Only two or three hours I hope. I plan on stopping by the Sky Lobby and asking Aunt Jenny to have lunch with me", Trina replied.

"That'll be so great. Tell her hi for me and that she needs to call me more often. After all, she is my baby sister." Trina laughed at her mother's remark. Her aunt looked much older than her mother did, so it was hard to picture her aunt as the baby sister.

"What do you know about this Mark who will be joining you? Does he live here on the island?" She glanced sideways at Trina trying to read her face while she waited for the answer.

Trina's reply came quick and nonchalantly. "All I can tell you is that he's only been at this school for a few months. He lives in New Jersey with his aunt and uncle because his parents are dead. I think someone said his parents died in a house fire or a car accident. I didn't really ask because I didn't want to pry. He seems very smart, and equally quiet. He has some friends, but not many. He is kind of a loner at school. I feel like I know him only because I see the look of hopelessness in his eyes. That makes me kind of understand where he is. I hope he'll be a great asset to the team and that I'll get to know him better, and yes, before you ask, he is very good looking." She saw the grin spread across her mother's face. Trina knew that Mark was not who her mother really wanted to ask her about so she volunteered the information.

"Don't forget that Lucas will be there as well. It's going seem strange to work with him again. We've not really talked since the accident. Of course, I haven't really given him much of a chance to talk with me. I've pretty much avoided him at all costs. Maybe this will be the way to open up a friendship with him again. I do NOT want to be his girlfriend again, but I would like to have his friendship. I think it's time to let old hurts go, if that's possible. I think with Mark there it just won't seem quite so awkward. At least I don't think it will be as awkward as it could be if it was only Lucas and I." Trina got a faraway look in her eyes. "Lucas seems so lost and lonely at school. He puts on a good front to his friends and teachers, but I know the real Lucas. He's still hurting. I hate to think that I'm part of the reason for that, but I know that I am."

Trina's mother interrupted her with her own question. "Were you aware that his mother called and asked if it was okay with your dad and I if Lucas was a part of this fundraiser?"

"I had no idea. Why would she wonder that? What did you say to her?"

"I told her if you were okay with it then I was okay with it. I think she believed we were upset with them because of the accident. I let her know that your dad and I had no bad feelings toward Lucas. After all, it was an accident. The Lucas we knew would never willingly hurt you. Besides, I think his father has punished him enough, don't you? I also believe he's still punishing himself. Therefore, maybe today will help him start down the road to forgiving himself. However, you need to know that Lucas' father doesn't know you are involved in this fundraiser. It seems that when you presented your idea to the teacher, and were waiting for his approval, that Lucas called his mother and told her about the idea. He wanted her opinion about joining in. She encouraged him, but they both agreed not to let his father know."

"Well what does his father think? Surely he doesn't think this was Lucas' idea." She tried to keep the anger out of her voice, but her mother could hear the change.

"His mother told his dad that Lucas was joining Mark in a fundraiser. When she told him where it was going to be held, he cut her off and asked no more questions. Since it was going to be at The Windows on the World Restaurant, he didn't need any more information about who was participating. I feel so sorry for the both of them. His dad seems like a nice enough man, but I think there are some areas in which he needs to improve. That's just my opinion, and best if kept between the two of us."

Trina laughed. She knew his father quite well. All fathers want what is best for their children. She supposed some parents just went overboard in trying to direct their children down that path. Lucas' father was a good example of that. She decided right then, and there, that she would give Lucas a chance at being friends again. She would try to leave the past in the past.

Trina's mother slowly pulled onto the ferry and parked on the lower level. She always stayed in her car for the ride across the river. Stepping up on deck make her feel queasy. After parking, she watched Trina get out of the car and walk to the upper deck just as she usually did. Reaching for her notes she prepared to read them for the meeting. She heard the squeal of tires as a car pulled onto the ferry. She glanced up as the car drove past her to the compact car section near the front. She instantly recognized the wavy blond hair. Lucas had just pulled into the spot and parked. He stepped out of his car and locked it, but did not seem to notice her. He walked up the same steps her daughter had just gone up, and she had to wonder if they would meet up on top, and if so, how it would turn out.

Trina stood at the rail looking out over the water. She loved the ferry. She loved the feel of the cool wind blowing over her, caressing her body. It did not matter if it was the middle of the summer, and the air was hot, or if it was the coldest winter day with an icy breeze. She loved it all. It was good think time. It was as if the wind could blow away all of her troubles. She did not really have many right now, but it helped to clear her head of whatever it was that made her feel uneasy. She was concerned with how many people they would eventually have sign up for this charity dinner. She had to give a final count to the executive chef at Windows on the World before she left the World Trade Center today. She thought of the few times she had been in the restaurant. She had only eaten at the restaurant a couple of times, but she loved it. The beauty of the New York skyline, especially at dusk, was an experience for the eyes that could not be put into proper words, no matter how one tried. The scene created its own poetry. The blue-black of the sky with all of the twinkling lights in the surrounding buildings made it seem like Christmas time all year long. She would just have to make sure that Mark and Lucas held up their end of the deal when it came to getting more commitments. Most of the work had been completed for them. She had gotten permission to distribute their letter and sign-up information, in the building. She had met with the executive chef to go over the menu and work out all of the details. She knew how much to charge so that they could raise a large amount of money. It helped that her father had been to several fundraiser events. Because of the location she was given permission to charge a thousand dollars a plate for this dinner. It was so generous of the chef and his staff to volunteer their time for this event. They had donated their wages for that night as their contribution to the event. She had targeted several major firms and sent them the information. She, Mark and Lucas were going to get the last few stragglers, collect their forms, and then she would meet with the chef.

The ferry landing came into sight and she knew it would only be a few minutes until they docked. She turned and headed back toward the stairs and her mother's car. Trina's mother looked at her inquisitively but said nothing. Trina opened the door and said nothing, so she figured Trina and Lucas had not met, or nothing had been said between them. They waited silently as the ferry docked, and then patiently pulled off the ferry. They drove around the tip of the island known as Battery Park, toward the Twin Towers to drop Trina off. As her mother pulled up and stopped, Trina opened the door and stepped out. She started to close the door when she had the strangest urge to speak to her mother. She popped her head back inside and looked lovingly at her mother sitting behind the steering wheel. Her mother, who had seemed so frazzled a short while before, sat completely composed behind the wheel of the car.

"Have I even bothered to tell you today that I think you're an awesome mother? I just want you to know that. I want you to always remember, no matter how busy your day gets, that I love you very much." With that said, she closed the door and walked away. Trina's mother sat there stunned. Suddenly she had the feeling that someone or some thing was squeezing the life out of her emotional heart. She had an eerie feeling that she would never see her daughter again. She chastised herself for such a ridiculous thought. After the crazy morning she'd had, she was just overcome with emotion by the remark her daughter had made. That was all it was, just a silly emotion. After all her daughter had been through, and survived, she knew that Trina was in God's hands and there was no safer place. She pulled away from the curb, and headed for her office in Midtown Manhattan.

# 3 Mark

Mark Jacobs repeatedly punched his pillow. He had heard his aunt call him loud and clear, and now she was threatening to come in and pull him out of bed. He knew she would not really enter his room to get him up. He hated the recurring feelings of anger toward his aunt when she would wake him each morning. He especially hated getting out of bed. This feeling was not because he hated school, school was okay. Actually, it was better than okay. He had always liked school. He challenged himself daily to do more than his best. School was the one piece of his life of which he felt he had total control. However, each morning that he woke up in his aunt and uncle's house was a reminder that he was alive and his parents were dead.

What he hated most of all, was eating breakfast with his aunt. He had been living with his aunt and uncle for the last six months. He loved both of them very much and knew that they loved him. They tried so hard to stay out of his way and give him breathing room. His problem was his aunt was his mother's twin sister. Every day when he looked at his aunt, he was constantly reminded of the mother he would never see again. It was almost unbearable. His aunt Tracy was the sweetest person on earth. She was his favorite aunt, and a very down to earth person. Her looks haunted him. Her facial features were identical to his mother's. There were some obvious differences. His aunt wore her wavy, auburn colored hair in a short cut just below the ears. His mother had always worn her hair about two inches above her shoulders, occasionally tying it up if she was cleaning house. It was his mother's belief that she always needed to look her best in case unexpected company showed up. She had been much taller than his aunt. While his mother had maintained a fine, trim figure, his aunt was shorter and a little on the plump side. Unlike his mother, she wore whatever was comfortable. On this day, as he sauntered into the kitchen, she happened to be wearing a pair of blue jeans and a short sleeved, button up blouse. This was something his mother would never have worn. Jeans were fine when they were camping, or she was working in her garden. She had always been the fashion conscious sister.

The major difference between his mother and his aunt, was the way they viewed life. His mother was always looking at the what ifs. What if someone unexpectedly showed up and her house was not spotless? What if someone came over and she was in grubby clothes? He remembered the day the neighbor had come over to return a rake and found his mother working in her flower garden. His mother had gone on and on apologizing for her appearance and the dirt on her jeans and hands. His aunt was the opposite. She was the type that could spill soup on her shirt and remark how clumsy she had been. Then she would shamelessly answer the door while wearing the same stained shirt. This is why he had spent so much time with his aunt each summer while he was growing up. His aunt was a rule breaker. It was the only time he was allowed to be a rule breaker. He did not need to always look his best. He could get dirty and not have to worry about it. He had the freedom to be a boy that sometimes came home dirty, or scraped up. He knew his mother had always wanted what was best for him. Now he would give anything to have her around to complain about the stains on his clothes.

The smile on his aunt's face was the same one he had seen at breakfast every day when his mother was alive. The look was one of love and pain. His aunt tried not to look him in the eyes as she placed a glass of milk on the table along with a bagel. She knew this would be all he would eat. It was all he had eaten every morning since coming to live with them. She remembered when Marks's mother was alive and he would come to visit her. He would spend the weekend or summers with her and practically eat her out of house and home. Breakfast usually consisted of two eggs, orange juice, milk, and a stack of pancakes. She would tease him, and tell him that if he continued to eat like a horse he would send them to the poor house. He would reply that she had to understand, he was a growing boy and needed all of her food. Besides, if they became poor then they would have to beg for the extra food he would need. His aunt would laugh at his reasoning. Since his parent's death, she felt he barely ate enough to keep going.

She knew he blamed himself for the fire, but she did not feel it was the right time to try to talk to him about the accident. The last time she had tried to talk to him about it, he had slammed out of the house and had not returned until late that night. They had looked all over the neighborhood. They called up the different game rooms, and places that other young people hung out. They had been unsuccessful in finding him. They had decided if he was not back by midnight they would consider him a runaway and call the police. He had returned a little before midnight. They said nothing to him that night. They had just let him sleep. It was only the next morning they had told him how scared they had been for him and his safety. He told them where he had gone. He had been only four blocks from the house. He had gone to the park up the street and sat on a bench feeding the squirrels and pigeons. When it had turned dark, he walked through the park for hours. He was thinking about how much he had hurt everyone. It seemed that all he could do was hurt people. He could not understand how they could take him into their house and love him after what he had done. After all, he had killed his parents. He had killed his aunt's only sister. They assured him of their love for him, and let him know that they had never blamed him for the accident. They were just so afraid they would lose him too. They let him know that it would have been unbearable if he had died in the fire. At least with him, they had a piece of what had been lost, to hold.

It was because of this incident, they had looked into putting him in Eagle Prep. It was far from his old school, and the prying, questioning eyes of his classmates. She knew there had been questions and remarks made, but nothing that he had mentioned. She had heard him one evening talking to someone on the phone about the kids at school whispering about the accident, and what had happened to his parents. She had overheard him say he wished that he were dead. They feared he would become so despondent he would attempt suicide. They had tried counseling but he refused to talk about that night. That is when they had made the decision to enroll him in Eagle Prep. Mark liked the school fine. He just thought his aunt and uncle's reason for putting him there was a little over the top. They had only been able to come up with twenty thousand dollars of the forty thousand dollar tuition. They applied for and received a scholarship for the rest. This was just one more thing about which he felt guilty. He knew his aunt and uncle had made sacrifices when they had taken him in. Now here he was the cause for another sacrifice. It seemed like all he was good for was causing more problems.

His aunt tried to make small talk at the table by reminding him that there was only three days until his eighteenth birthday. She asked him, "Is there anything special you want to do on your special day?" Instead of answering her, Mark picked up the bagel and began to spread strawberry flavored cream cheese on it, letting the silence in the room grow. He hated the strawberry cream cheese, yet he ate it anyway. He remembered the first time his mom had bought the strawberry flavored cream cheese. He had argued with her for five minutes about it. She wanted him to taste it and he insisted it would be gross. He finally bit into the bagel to shut her up. Then he made the biggest mistake by lying to her and telling her it was great. She had handed him the bagel and he had to eat the whole thing, or admit he had lied. Now he sat there eating it because it had been her favorite.

Mark picked up his dirty dishes and put them into the sink, and went to brush his teeth. As he looked into the mirror, the reflection that stared back at him was that of his father when he was Mark's age. Everyone was always telling him how much he looked like his dad. He had seen pictures of his father when he was in his twenties. His father had been of average height, five foot nine, with an average weight of one hundred and sixty pounds. He'd had wavy brown hair that was beginning to gray at the temples, and deep, dark brown eyes. His mustache made him look older than he was. What impressed Mark so much about his father were his muscles. His arms were well muscled from working for years in the field of construction. As Mark looked into the mirror, he realized he truly was the spitting image of his dad, right down to the muscles he was developing. He did not yet possess the mustache his father had worn. His father had always worked on one of the skyscrapers under construction in Manhattan. He was proud that he could say his father had worked at the World Trade Center after the bomb went off in the parking garage, in February of 1993. He had always wanted to be just like him. That is why he worked out every day trying to build his muscles. His father had told him several times that he wanted him to go to college and be so much more than he was. Mark saw nothing wrong with what his father had become. He loved him for his humility.

Mark pulled back from the mirror. He could feel the anger rising in him again. It was not fair. He should have died in the fire, not his parents. He grabbed his toothbrush and toothpaste and scrubbed his teeth trying to work through the anger. When he had finished, he left the bathroom and stomped to the front room. Grabbing his backpack, he sprinted to the door past his aunt so he would not have to speak to her. He knew that these feelings of anger usually caused him to behave in a manner that most people considered rude. He also knew that no matter what, his aunt and uncle understood that he loved them and respected them. They knew that he was trying to find his way back to them. Sometimes he felt like he was in the deepest, darkest hole with no way out. He needed them. They were his lifelines and he was theirs. The hole was deeper some days than others. He felt like he was suffocating. He just wanted the nightmare to end.

Mark walked the eight blocks to the PATH train station that would take him to the World Trade Center. When his parents were alive, he would ride the red line train from Newark, New Jersey to Manhattan. Now he took the blue line train from Hoboken to the World Trade Center and then switched lines to take him to his school. Nothing much changed. It was a different line and different people but the ride was the same, boring. It gave him more time to think about how he had screwed up his life and the life of those in his family. Mark switched gears and thought about what he would do if he reached the mall under the Trade Centers before the others arrived. He decided he could do some shopping before meeting up with Trina. Maybe he could buy a present for his aunt to make up for the way he had treated her that morning. He always felt racked with guilt over the way he treated her. He never set out to intentionally hurt her. If was like a defense mechanism.

Trina was the reason that he had volunteered for this community service. He had heard that she had close connections with the Angels Hope charity. He hoped that by giving back to the community, and especially to burn victims, that he would not feel quite so guilty that he was alive. It may have been the wrong reason for helping but at this point, he felt that this would help him get past the guilt that he felt every waking moment, of every day, of his life. He needed to find the courage to face the accident and accept the permanent changes in his life. Most importantly, he needed to learn how to forgive himself. This is where he felt the most lost.

# 4 Lucas

Lucas James was up early as usual. His father had insisted that they eat breakfast at the country club. Although the food at the country club was great, he drank only a cup of coffee. He hated the atmosphere in the country club. The place was always full of older people. Most of the young people who attended on a regular basis were just like his dad, snobby. His dad told him people like this would hire him one day. His dad just didn't get it. He did not want people like these men hiring him. He felt they were old, with outdated ideas. He had always liked being in a family where money seemed to be no problem. There were definitely more benefits to having money than not having it. However, the ideals of his father and his father's friends were not necessarily his. He had lived under his father's rule for years. If he did something wrong, according to his father, it was always the other person's fault. Don't ever blame one of his family members. This was just one of many things he and his father did not agree on. He still felt guilty for the accident that had injured his former girlfriend Trina. What made him feel so guilty was that his father had hired someone to track down the motorcyclist who had pulled out in front of him. A partner in his dad's law firm pinned the accident on the motorcyclist. Lucas walked away from the accident with some broken bones, an increase in his insurance policy, and the loss of driving privileges for two weeks. That is exactly how long it took his dad to buy him a new car. The only real thing of value he had lost due to the accident was Trina. His father was the reason that they were no longer together. When he had visited the hospital with his son and seen the hideous burns that covered her legs, he knew he could never let his son continue in the relationship. He feared his friends from the country club would see Trina sitting on the front of his yacht. What would everyone think? They might ban him from the country club. Worse, yet, they might truly think that the accident was his son's fault and that they were keeping her around out of pity. Lucas had argued values with his father once before. He learned very quickly that what his father said, you did without question. His father had made it clear to him that as long as he lived under his roof he would live by his rules and his values. That meant his father chose his friends, his projects, and tied it all together with money. There would be no money now, or in the future if Lucas did not do as he was told. He was not sure that he wanted the money. The price now seemed to be too high. His father's recent decisions were intruding on his future. He just needed to decide how he was going to stand up to his father, and when. He needed to find the courage somewhere, and he needed to do it soon. College was approaching. He needed to figure out if his father was going to help pay for it, or if he was going to handle it on his own.

According to his father, one of the lowest jobs you could ever have would be that of a teacher. He followed the old adage, "those who can- do and those who can't – teach." How could he tell his dad that he really wanted to be a high school P.E teacher and coach?    Helping kids strengthen their bodies and make healthy choices, coaching and teaching them how to be a team player was what he wanted to do with his life. Many attributes, such as being a team player, were missing in his life. His father wanted him on his team, yet his own father had never been a team player. His dad wanted him to work on Wall Street, be a doctor, or a lawyer like himself. These were positions that his father considered respectable and prestigious. Nothing was respectable about being a teacher, as far as his father was concerned. As much as he liked the money and what he could do with it, he wondered if it mattered having it if you were unhappy. He often wondered if his mother felt the same way he did.

His mother had been a dancer. His father met her at a ballet where she was the prima ballerina.   He had followed her around from performance to performance, until she finally agreed to go to dinner with him. After a very short courtship they married, and that was the end of her dancing career. According to his father, a good wife stayed home, had the cook bake cookies for her, while she attended important social committees. His mother was consistently reminded of her place in the household. He could look at his mother and see that she was not very happy.

She resigned herself to be a good wife. Once she had been an independent person who knew who she was and what she wanted in life. After her marriage, she was often bored and felt useless and worthless. She no longer had a purpose in life, except for Lucas. She saw how her husband treated their son. He claimed he wanted the best for Lucas. She had tried to tell him that he was going about it in the wrong way. He claimed to know what was best for his son, just as if he knew what was best for her. That was why he had insisted that she quit dancing. She just sighed and tried to soothe Lucas when he and his father butted heads. When attending the ballet, Lucas would see the faraway look in his mother's eyes. A look that told him she would rather be up on stage than in the audience. He knew that she was picturing herself as the main character in the performance. Lucas knew that if there was some way he could change their lives, he would.

Lucas finished his coffee and told his father he had to leave. His father made a big display of telling his son goodbye. He made sure everyone within hearing distance knew that his son was meeting some important people downtown to organize a one thousand dollar plate fundraiser. Lucas just shook his head in disbelief and walked out of the country club tremendously embarrassed. It would not have been so bad if his father really believed in what Lucas was doing. His father cared only about the fact they were setting up the fundraiser at Windows on the World and that it cost one thousand dollars a plate. He didn't really care that the money raised would help the organization that had been beneficial in helping Trina move on with her life after the accident.

Lucas walked quickly out the door and handed the valet his ticket. The valet pulled up in his red Corvette. Lucas hopped in and sped off toward the Staten Island Ferry. He drove onto the ferry a few minutes before it was ready to depart. After parking in one of the compact car spots he headed for the upper deck. He and Trina used to stand at the front rail looking out over the water. He missed those days. He had dated a few people but no one more than once or twice. He just could not forget what he had done.

On the upper deck, he walked around taking in the sites. As they began to pull away from the pier, he saw a familiar face. He took a couple of steps back to make sure she could not see him. Trina was leaning against the rail, her beautiful long hair was pulled back and held by a barrette. The long hair hanging down her back looked beautiful blowing in the wind. His heart began to ache. He could never forgive himself for the terrible thing she had overheard him say. She would not even let him explain what had truly happened. He had been arguing with his father. He had finally given in, and was screaming what his father had wanted to hear. As he became angry, his voice had risen and she had overheard a portion of the conversation. He had felt terrible about hurting her again. He figured she would be better off without him around. He never did explain what had actually been said that day. Every day that he saw her at school was another day he felt guilty. He volunteered for this assignment only because Trina was heading it. Since the accident, she had not talked to him. Oh, she was very polite to him. If she was in a group with him, she would participate. They were never alone together so that he could talk with her about that night. She made sure of that. She said the obligatory "hi" to him as she passed him in the hall. Lucas hung his head as he thought about the situation. He would try to do a good job on this assignment. Maybe, just maybe it would restore their friendship. He could ask for no more. He quietly walked back down to his car and sat inside. He waited for the ferry to dock. As soon as they let the cars off, Lucas headed toward the World Trade Center. He pulled into the underground parking area. He locked up his car and headed for the mall. With any luck, he would run into Mark first. He figured it would be an easier icebreaker if he were with Mark when Trina arrived.

# 5 The Meeting

Mark stepped out of the subway terminal under the south tower of the World Trade Center, and entered the mall. As he walked toward the Coffee Station, his mind wandered to thoughts of Trina. He had seen her around school. She was in his Biology and English Literature class. A beautiful girl, she seemed kind of quiet and locked inside herself at times. He found this hard to understand because he had heard she had been a cheerleader. Everyone knew that cheerleaders were the most outgoing people around. He had also heard she no longer cheered because of an accident. He could see no physical reason for her not to cheer. He knew all too well how crippling a bad event in your life could be. He had heard that Lucas had been her boyfriend at the time and dropped her because of the accident. If he had been the old Mark, he would have called Lucas a jerk. Since the fire, he decided it was best not to judge anyone. He was not walking in their shoes and he did not know all of the details, so he had no right to think anything bad. Lucas was in his Calculus class. By all rights, he seemed to be an okay person. You would think that someone with his money would be stuck up. He had often heard people say that Lucas was a snob, but he had never seen that side of him. Maybe it was just jealous gossip. On many occasions, he had seen Lucas slip someone money for lunch, even if these people had not asked for it. He was creative, saying he had found a five dollar bill behind their chair, and he knew it had to belong to them because he'd already asked everyone else, and it wasn't his. Somehow he seemed to really care about others.

Mark decided to grab a quick cup of coffee and see if Lucas or Trina had arrived yet. He headed for the Coffee Station. As he approached, he saw Lucas coming from the other direction and waved to him. They met in front of the station and shook hands. It felt like the thing they should do; yet, at the same time it felt strange. They did not know each other well enough to high five each other, or say 'what's up man'. Mark ordered a cup of coffee with light cream and sugar and Lucas ordered an iced cappuccino. They found a small table and sat down.

Lucas decided to break the awkward silence. "So, where did you go to school before Eagle Prep?"

"I went to school at Watts High in Newark. When my parents died, I went to live with my aunt and uncle. They were afraid that I wasn't adjusting well, so they put me in Eagle Prep."

That was true. He had not told Lucas to what it was they were afraid he was not adjusting. He used the excuse that his aunt had asked for suggestions, and changed the subject. He mentioned that he had a birthday coming in three days.

"Listen! I really don't want to spend my birthday with my aunt and uncle. Got any good suggestions? The water's beginning to get too cold to go to the beach."

"Yeah man, why don't you come to my house for your birthday? I'll throw you a party. We have a pool, and I can invite a few of the kids from school." Lucas waited for a reply that didn't come.

Mark wasn't sure if Lucas had said this trying to impress him, or if he really wanted to throw a party for him. Lucas immediately understood the hesitation and put Mark's mind at ease.

"Look Mark, you're fairly new at school and don't really have a lot of friends. This will be a great way for you to meet them and get to know some of the other kids. So what do you say?"

"Okay. That sounds great. What would you like me to bring?

"Just bring your swim trunks and yourself. I'll provide all of the food, drinks and fun. I'll ask about ten or twelve kids that are in some of the same classes with us. I'll tell you what, I'll even pick you up."

"Lucas, are you nuts? I live in New Jersey."

"Hey, not a problem, I have a couple of friends that I'll invite who live in Hoboken like you.

"How are you going to fit all of us into your Corvette?"

Lucas began to laugh. "Unfortunately, one of the downsides to having money is that I have three vehicles; a Corvette, truck and a van."

Mark laughed with Lucas then asked, "How could having money have a downside?"

The smile faded from Lucas' face before he answered. "You know, everyone thinks it's the greatest thing having a family with all of this money. However, imagine if you will, you come home one day and your dad says, 'happy sixteenth birthday son. I have a surprise. I have a new truck for you in case you need to haul anything in the future. Oh, by the way, we're having an apartment built on to the house, so you can have some privacy'. Then he walks back into the house and that's the end of your birthday. There was no cake, no friends, no special dinner, nothing. You know, he had that apartment finished in three weeks. He called in special favors to get all of the permits and inspecting done. He hired people to work around the clock. I came home from school to find all of my things from my old room already moved out into my new apartment."

"Whoa, that would be awful." Mark was at a loss for words.

"You want to hear a really good one? He keeps my refrigerator stocked so that I can have all the friends over I want as long as I let the parents know in advance. That way we won't have a conflict in our schedules. For my seventeenth birthday he bought me a van in case I wanted to go somewhere with a large group of friends. We get along as long as I stay in my part of the house, and he stays in his. He's out many evenings, so my mom comes out and eats with me. Once a week he insists we go have breakfast at his stupid country club. I don't know if this is what he considers quality father – son time, bonding or what. I think he hopes all of his friends will have an influence on me or else I'll take an interest in their business."

Mark did not know what to think. He figured he had it much better than Lucas did in many ways. It sounded as if Lucas' father only cared about appearances and what others thought. It probably gave him great pleasure to tell his friends that his son had his own apartment.

Mark tried to change the subject. " So, what are your plans when you graduate?"

Lucas laughed, "That's another story. My father's plan for my life was to have me go to college and become a lawyer, doctor, or work on Wall Street. Any of those 'respectable' jobs would do. Then I told him what I really wanted to do. From the time I was in middle school, I've wanted to teach high school PE and be a coach. One afternoon I made the mistake of coming home, and telling this to my father. He said, no son of his would ever work at such a loser job because, 'those who could did and those who couldn't taught'. That was one of his favorite lines. He would support the coaches for the teams I played on, but there was no way his son would be a coach."

Mark felt terrible for Lucas. His parents, while they were alive, and his aunt and uncle believed he should be whatever he wanted to be. They were willing to help him achieve that goal at all cost. Before Lucas could ask Mark any more questions they were startled by Trina's sudden appearance. She had stood off to the side watching and listening to Mark and Lucas, before approaching. When she had seen Lucas and his blond wavy hair, her stomach had begun to turn flips. She was nervous. She remembered how blue his eyes were and how muscular his body was. Her heart ached, for days gone by. As she approached, she remarked to her two partners, "I didn't know that you two knew each other."

Both of them jumped, startled by her sudden appearance. Mark answered, "We don't really, we're in the same Calculus class.

Lucas quickly asked, "Would you like a cup of your usual latte?"

"Sure." She was surprised he had remembered.

As Lucas went to the counter to order, Trina took the opportunity to talk with Mark. "I know we have some classes together", she commented, "but we never really talk. How do you like it at Eagle Prep?"

"Actually, it isn't as bad as I thought it would be. I like a challenge. It's probably one of the best things that my aunt and uncle could have done for me. The cost is a little much, but I plan on paying my aunt and uncle back." Lucas returned with Trina's latte. As he handed it to her he cleared his throat, drew a deep breath, and plunged in.

"Look Trina, I don't expect you to understand or believe anything I tell you. However, I want this project to go well. I hope you know that and believe it. I also hope you will at least forgive me enough that we can work together, and maybe sometime in the future we can be friends again."

Trina was shocked. She had been afraid that he would say something awful to her and here he was apologizing to her. She looked at him and nonchalantly replied, "Consider it done." Her cool demeanor didn't show the turmoil going on inside of her.

Mark was not sure what had just happened, but he felt the tension that surrounded them leave. "Well, what's the game plan today?"

Trina thought for a minute. "Why don't we divide and conquer. I have an aunt that works in the sky lobby. I want to check in with her to see if she would like to go to lunch with me after we are done. Would either of you like to join us?"

Mark and Lucas looked at each other and Lucas quickly said, "Thanks for the offer, but I told Mark I would treat him to lunch today. We're planning his birthday party for this weekend. It's kind of a way to introduce him to other people at the school." Mark just smiled and went along with what Lucas had said. He'd thank him later for getting him out of an awkward situation. He didn't know Trina well enough yet. That didn't mean he didn't find her fascinating or dream of asking her out one day. It was just that today was not that day.

33

Trina smiled and nodded. "Well then, let's get started. Mark, why don't you go to the eighty-eighth floor and meet with Mr. Morrow from Saddler, Kimchi, and Morrow Investments. He has a list of employees and clients that have agreed to pay a thousand dollar fee for the dinner and we need to get the list. Make sure that everyone has filled out the proper forms and that there is a form for every name on the list. I'll go to the sky lobby on the seventy-eighth floor, and see if I can't go from office to office and talk some more clients into joining us. Besides, I need to see if my aunt wants to go to lunch with me. Lucas, will you go to the South Tower? Check with your father's firm and some of the other attorneys, maybe we will have some luck. They received the information and I know your father signed up for the charity dinner but we haven't heard from some of the others on that floor. Make sure to stop at some of the other offices on the sixty-fifth floor to see if they were aware of the fundraiser. Here is a set of forms and the paper on which to list their names. What do you say we meet back here at ten and go over what we've accomplished? That way we'll know what we have to do next. I'll try to get up to Windows on the World, and we'll finalize menu plans. If we can get three hundred people to sign up for this, we'll have made three hundred thousand dollars for the "Angels Hope Charity."

Trina checked her watch. It was eight thirty. That would give them a little less than an hour and a half to cover as many offices as possible. It wasn't as if they were going to go from office to office and say, 'Hi, I'm collecting money for a charity, would you like to make a donation'. That would have been easy. First, they would have to explain what the Angels Hope benefit was. Then they would have to explain why it was important for them to participate in this benefit. A long time ago, she had learned there was a difference between someone giving to a charity out of pity, and someone giving because it tugged at their heartstrings. She wanted the latter, but she would take anyone, even someone like Lucas' father who would give just so he could say, 'see what I did, aren't you proud of me for giving so much money?' Everyone would really know he did not care about the charity. He cared only about looking good in other people's eyes.

After her accident, he had donated money to the burn center. He claimed it was because he really cared about people like her, and since he knew her personally, it brought it closer to his heart. She knew better than that. He had never once come to see her and as far as she knew, he did not even have a heart. She knew that thought was very cold. She was not quite ready to forgive him yet.

# 6 Countdown to Terror

Trina and Mark watched Lucas head through the mall toward the South Tower. As they walked toward the elevators, they chatted.

" So tell me Trina, what else do you do besides organize fund raiser?"

Laughing she replied, " Actually I hate doing fund raisers. It was my aunt's idea. She figured with all of the time and effort that would be put into the fund raiser, we would have over half of our community service hours right at the beginning of the school year, and we could always work in one of the soup kitchens on weekends or holidays, to complete our twenty-five hours."

Mark laughed. He was seeing another side to this girl he thought was so quiet. He could tell there was an underlying strength to her, and he wondered where it came from. They entered the elevator and headed for the forty-fourth floor, the location of the first sky lobby. There they could get on another elevator that would take them to other floors or the next sky lobby. Trina noticed Mark checking her out.

"Okay, what gives? Do I have my shirt on backwards or something?" Mark turned red. He had not realized he had been so obvious. He had been thinking that she would probably be a fun date, if he ever got up the nerve to ask her out.

He quickly checked himself. "No, I was just wondering something."

"Like what?"

"Well, it's kind of personal and maybe a little prying."

"Don't worry, I've had all kinds of prying questions asked of me in the past few years and it really doesn't bother me anymore", she lied.

"Okay, well I'd heard when I came to this school, that you had been a cheerleader until you had an accident. I was wondering why you don't cheer anymore. You look like you're in great shape to me. Did your parents make you quit?"

Trina let out her breath. She had not realized she was holding it. She was so used to people asking her the particulars about the accident, and at times, it still bothered her. He was not asking for particulars. She found it a little amusing. It was almost as if he was sizing her up to ask her for a date. Was he testing the waters? Did she want him to ask her out on a date? She had dated no one since her accident.

She smiled at him, "Oh trust me, my parents encouraged me to go back to cheerleading. My injuries had taken such a long time to heal, and I had suffered some broken bones, and some burns. During my recovery I realized how shallow I had been, and that it was time to focus on other things." She could not tell Mark that she was afraid that people would stare at her and focus only on her scars if she started to cheer again. The answer seemed to satisfy Mark.

"Okay, my turn to ask you prying questions", she said with a giggle.

"Go ahead."

"I understand that you live with your aunt and uncle because you lost your parents. Did you lose them in a car accident."

Mark had told no one what had happened to his parents. He wasn't even sure if the Dean of the school knew, and if he did, how much he knew.

"No, there was a fire at my house. I woke up and found my room engulfed in flames. The only way out was through my bedroom window. I ran around to the front of the house to get my parents out but it was too late. My parents were deaf, and according to the fire investigation, the equipment that would have turned the lights on with the smoke detector didn't work. They never had a chance. They found them in their bed dead from smoke inhalation. It was entirely my fault that they died, and I lived."

Trina knew that people often felt guilty about things they had no control over. She had felt that way after her accident, so she thought she understood.

Mark left Trina at the sky lobby and took another elevator up to the eighty-eighth floor. He stepped off the elevator and moved down the hallway. He stopped outside the offices of Saddler, Kimchi, and Morrow and took a deep breath. He knew that this was a big opportunity for him. He was glad to volunteer for this assignment. He hoped that one day he would be able to work for an investment firm like this. It was important that he make a good impression, because they might be the one to hire him in the future. That kind of success would make his aunt and uncle happy. It was not just the idea that he could make good money. His parents had always worked hard to make sure he had everything he needed, and tried to give him some of the things he wanted. They wanted him to strive to reach his dreams. He had always loved Manhattan, and envisioned himself in an office in one of these very towers. He opened the door to the office and stepped up to the receptionist desk. The secretary looked up and smiled.

"Hi, I'm Mark Jacobs and I have an appointment with Mr. Morrow. "

"Welcome Mark, my name is Margie. If you'll have a seat I'll let Mr. Morrow know that you're here." She stepped to the large ornate door to the left of her desk, knocked and went inside. She had been inside for approximately five minutes when she stepped back out. She held the door for Mark and ushered him in.

Mark stepped into the office and took a good look around. He had never been in such a grand office. Mr. Morrow's office was spacious. He had a sofa against one wall. In front of the sofa was a coffee table with a silver tray and coffee pot on it. Across from it were two armchairs. The soft rose-colored sofa and chairs complimented the deep burgundy colored carpet. Bookshelves lined the other wall and they were full of books. The two chairs in front of his desk were as large and plush as the two armchairs across from the couch, and of the same color. Mr. Morrow's desk, like his bookshelves and other furniture was made of beautiful mahogany wood. It was the largest desk that Mark had ever seen. He figured that four people of small to average size could work at it with plenty of elbow room. Mr. Morrow stood up and shook hands with him, then asked him to sit down. Mark was speechless as he looked at the view from Mr. Morrow's office. It seemed as if he could see all the way into midtown Manhattan. What person would not want a view like this? He could only hope that one day he would have an office half as nice as this one, with such a gorgeous view. As Mr. Morrow sat in his chair, Mark had a chance to size him up. He seemed to be a very confident and unshakable person. His hair was thinning. His skin was very pale from being indoors so much. His looks coupled with his black silk suit and red power tie gave Mark a quick impression that he was sitting across from a mortician. Mark turned his head to stifle a laugh. He knew it was not really an appropriate thought. Mr. Morrow quickly glanced at his watch. It was eight forty-five.

"Well Mark, I can only give you fifteen minutes because I have a meeting at nine. Mark straightened up in his chair to begin his conversation with Mr. Morrow. Instead of speaking, he stared past Mr. Morrow without answering him. He was sure his eyes were mistaken. He stared in horrified disbelief at what he thought – no, what he knew he saw tearing across the sky toward the building. He screamed and pointed toward the windows.

Mr. Morrow whirled around in his chair to see what Mark was staring at. What could have caused such an emotional outburst? What he saw made his stomach lurch. Heading straight toward the towers was a plane. It was not just any plane. There had always been the fear that a small plane might veer off course and hit the Twin Towers, but no one could ever imagine the size of the airliner he saw racing toward his building. The inevitable impact occurred less than a minute later. It was above

Mr. Morrow's office by several floors. A horrible explosion rocked the entire building. The building twisted, then swayed from side to side for about ten seconds. The building began to creak and crack as it undulated. The force threw Mark to the floor. He was sure that he and Mr. Morrow were dead. After the swaying and vibrations in the building stopped Mark stood up. The eerie quiet was disturbing. He rushed to the window to see if he could see anything. Suddenly he wished he had not. A flaming, arm flailing body, plummeted past the window. Immediately he knew, he was going to be sick. He turned to the wastebasket and vomited. Mr. Morrow handed him a tissue.

"We have get out of the office", he cried. Mark looked at him and realized that the event was so horrific that the unshakeable and confident Mr. Morrow had wet himself. He was sure of one thing at that moment, they needed to leave the building immediately. As they left the office Mr. Morrow grabbed Margie. She was searching for her purse. He told her to leave it as they headed for the stairs. As they ran they noticed the ceiling was missing in several areas. Wires hanging down from the ceiling were giving off sparks. Small fires had been ignited throughout the offices. They stepped into Stairway "A" leaving the eighty-eighth floor behind.

The first thing that Mark noticed as they entered the stairway was how hot it was. By the time they had calmly gone down three floors he was completely drenched in sweat. He took off his school blazer and left it on the stair rail. He figured if everything turned out okay, he could always come back to get it, and if not, he would either buy a new one, or he would not need one. His only concern now was getting out alive. He wondered if Trina had felt the same thing he had. Did she know what had happened? Was she safe and evacuating the building? As he continued down the stairs, they met up with other people from other floors. As more people entered the congested stairway, things began to slow down. He was surprised at how calm most everyone appeared to be. Were they in shock he wondered, or was this the way they were trained to evacuate. He also wondered how long it would take them to go down eighty-eight floors. He knew before the plane hit, that Trina had been ten floors beneath him. Had she rushed out immediately? Was she lying hurt somewhere? These thoughts consumed him as he made his way down one slow, agonizing flight of stairs after another.

# 7 The Nightmare

Trina stepped off the elevator onto the seventy-eighth floor sky lobby with Mark. Since it was his first visit up here, she pointed out the elevator he would need to take him to the eighty-eighth floor. She watched him walk toward the elevator, get on and wave at her as the doors closed. Her aunt was one of several receptionists for the many offices on that floor. This was the floor where people transferred to elevators that would take them to other floors. Trina walked across the lobby to the receptionist's desk. She saw her aunt sitting with her telephone headset on. She had on her beautiful blue suit. It was one of Trina's favorites. The color reminded her of a robin's egg. Trina noticed her aunt's blond hair pulled back like her own. She had purposely dressed to emulate her aunt. She walked up to the desk and stood quietly in front. Her aunt knew that someone was standing in front of her and asked if she could help before looking up.

"I thought maybe I could help you", Trina replied with a big smile on her face. Her aunt looked up in surprise and squealed, "What are you doing here? Aren't you supposed to be in school?"

She jumped up, threw off her headset, and ran around the desk to hug her niece. The plush carpet and her heels made it difficult to run, but she did her best. She grabbed Trina and hugged her for several seconds. Stepping back, she took a good look at her niece and began to giggle.

"I see my great fashion sense has rubbed off on you."

"I figured since I was coming here to urge people to give me their hard earned money, I might as well look reputable. I'm here to finalize the details for the fundraiser and to invite you to lunch afterwards. I thought we could go to the cafeteria on the forty-third floor."

"Sounds like a plan to me. I take my lunch at eleven, is that okay with you?"

"That will be great because I need to meet up with Mark and Lucas at ten."

"Are we talking about Lucas James?"

"The very one."

"Your parents approved of this meeting?" she queried.

"Sure. Lucas volunteered because he wanted to do the fundraiser, and he just wanted to try to be friends again. His mother called mom to see if it was okay, and she said she was fine with it. The only thing that Lucas' mother asked was that no-one tell her husband that he was going to be doing the fund raiser with me."

"You know, it's terrible that Lucas has to sneak around to do something right just because his father's an idiot. So, tell me, who is this Mark character you mentioned. Boyfriend maybe?"

"He's just a guy that's in my Biology and English Lit classes. He seems kind of a loner. He lost his parent in a fire and lives with his aunt and uncle in Hoboken. He's very nice, and r-e-a-l cute. As a matter of fact, he was checking me out in the elevator. I thought he might be getting up the courage to ask me out. Maybe he will before the day is over. I think it's time I got back into the dating game." Trina realized she was rattling but couldn't stop herself. She was definitely nervous when it came to thinking about getting back into the dating game.

"Wow! That's my girl. It is time you took the next step. I know it's been hard on you. You've not felt sure enough about yourself to allow anyone to get too close to you. I told your mom if she'd give you enough room and time to figure it out on your own you'd be okay."

"Thanks for the vote of encouragement. Are you telling me my mother asked you for advice, her baby sister?"

Her aunt laughed and replied, "I may be the baby in the family but I am the one with all of the common sense and brains."

Trina stepped behind the desk with her aunt. "Well, mom said to tell you that you should call more often." She sat down in one of the many chairs behind the desk next to her aunt. Suddenly there was a terrible explosion and a violent shaking of the building. The twisting sounded like spaghetti snapping when you break it to put it into a pot of boiling water. At the same time the building shook; the elevator doors opened and people began to enter. There was a terrible whooshing sound coming down the elevator shaft. The sound of rushing air and a ball of fire shot out into the lobby. Trina's aunt grabbed her and threw her under the desk. The sudden overly heated air shattered windows sucking those closest to them out. Papers ignited and the extreme heat began to melt the carpet. As Trina and her aunt tried to stand up the computer shook from the desk, and hit her aunt in the head causing a deep gash and knocking her semi-conscious. The floor felt as if it was buckling. Trina could hear terrible screams. Trina slowly stood up and looked around.

She had stood up in time to see people from the elevator running past her engulfed in flames. Their skin bubbled up then seemed to drip from their bones. They fell just a few feet beyond her. She knew they were dead. Inhaling the flames and extremely heated smoke and air had caused a quick death for many. Several people had been standing a few feet from the elevator and suffered terrible burns from the flames that had shot down the elevator shaft. This is where most of the screams came from. Many of these people ran past her plummeting out the windows to certain death. She knew that the desk had protected both her and her aunt. There were scorch marks along the front of it. Trina screamed. She was living her nightmare all over again.

A nightmare was what she had lived almost two years before. She had been with her boyfriend Lucas. They had just won the state soccer game and the coach had invited the team and the cheerleaders to his house for a victory party. It seemed like the perfect night. She, the cheerleading captain was out with her boyfriend, the soccer team captain. Trina and Lucas mingled with the other guests. She sat on a couch with a group of her friends talking.

"So Trina, are you and Lucas going to the victory dance together?"

Trina looked at Suzie, her co-captain. "Wouldn't that be the perfect ending to a perfect night if he asked me? He hasn't yet but I'm sure he will. Why, do you know something I don't?

Suzie giggled. "A little birdie told me Lucas was going to ask you after the game tonight."

Trina looked around the room for Lucas. "That little birdy wouldn't happen to be Jerry, would it? Someone told me he's already asked you."

"Of course. He didn't want to take a chance someone else would grab hold of this fine body and take his spot." Suzie laughed along with the other girls. She was so fun to be around.

"What about you Tracy, are you going with Thomas?"

Tracy smiled at Trina, "Haven't you heard? Thomas is old news. Leo asked me and I said yes. You know what they say; 'you snooze you lose', and Thomas just lost."

Trina looked around for the boys. Where did they get off to? She stood up deciding to find Lucas. The coach's house wasn't very large. There was only one floor so she should have been able to spot Lucas. She walked from room to room looking for him. She found several of the guys in the game room with the coach shooting pool. Lucas wasn't in there. The only other place she could think he might have gone was out on the patio. There was a pool out there and several kids had decided to sit around the fire pit out there. She couldn't find him anywhere. She went back in and joined her friends. It was an hour before Trina finally saw him. She just assumed he, Jerry and Leo had been outside talking. She was beginning to get tired. It had been a busy day. First, they had their regular school day and the pep rally, and finally the game. All she wanted to do was go home and sleep. She felt like she could probably sleep for days. She asked Lucas to take her home. She hugged Tracy and Suzie goodbye. They had only been in the car for a few minutes when she realized something was wrong. Lucas, who was usually very talkative, was very quiet and appeared to be extremely sleepy or sluggish. He drifted toward the edge of the road. Trina mentioned this to him. He kind of laughed and moved back into his lane. It was then she realized he had been drinking.

"Lucas, stop and let me out. I'll call my dad and he can come get me."

"Hey, I'm not drunk. I can take you home."

"Please Lucas, just pull over and let me out. You know how I feel about being in the car with someone who's been drinking. Just stop and let me out, please."

"Look, Jerry, Leo and I only had one beer. Leo had brought it from his house. What was I going to do, say no thanks?"

She had never known him to drink anything. In fact, he had always been against it. He said his father did plenty of it. He was not a drunk or an alcoholic, but Lucas did not like the way his father talked down to him when he'd had a couple of drinks in him. This is why it surprised her that he'd been drinking.

As they rounded the next curve, a motorcycle pulled out from a side road. Even though there was no danger of him striking the motorcycle, in his slightly impaired state he panicked and jerked the steering wheel hard to the right. The car jumped a ditch, ran through a barbed wire fence, and flipped end over end three times. Lucas flew out on the first flip and landed hard in the dirt. He knew immediately that he had broken something. The pain was unrelenting. He called out to Trina, but was unable to move to get to her. He knew he needed to get to her, to protect or help her. It was amazing how sobering an accident could be.

Trina was not as lucky as Lucas. On the second flip of the car the passenger door flew open and the force propelled Trina ahead of the car. She landed in the dirt with the full force of the car crashing down upon her. She was pinned from below her chest. The pain was excruciating. Slowly, the breath was being crushed out of her. She knew she was going to die. Then, there was a loud "whoosh." The gas tank had ruptured spilling gasoline on the ground, sending it running toward the hot engine. Trina began to lose consciousness due to a lack of oxygen. She felt the hot metal and flames licking at her body. She didn't even have enough breath to scream. Her last thought was, 'please God make it quick'. Unconsciousness overtook her before the flames began to ravage her body. The skin on her legs began to blister. An off duty officer following behind the car witnessed the accident and called in for help.

Seeing the flames, the officer knew he had to get the young girl away from the car. As he approached with his fire extinguisher, he noticed the car was lying on top of her and flames were greedily licking at her body. He sprayed the burning grass around her aware he would not be able to extinguish the fire blazing in the engine and burning her body. He ran to his car and grabbed a jack. He jammed it under the edge of the car and pumped the handle as fast as he could pump it, lifting the car just enough to pull her out. He knew she needed airlifted to the nearest hospital. He called dispatch and asked for a Life Flight helicopter. As he brushed the hair from her face to begin assessing her injuries, he gasped. He knew this girl. Her parents were his best friends. With the weight of the car gone, Trina began to breathe shallowly. He begged her to hang on, telling her that help was only a matter of minutes away. He briefly left her lying in the damp grass and went to check on the young man.

Lucas was in a lot of pain. He kept asking for Trina. Yelling for her, he kept telling the officer that he had to help her. He told Lucas to lie still, that the paramedics were on their way. He went back to wait with Trina and encourage her to hang on. When the paramedics arrived, he directed them to the two injured teens. As the paramedics readied Lucas for the ambulance, Life Flight arrived to take Trina to the hospital. They stabilized her as much as possible, and placed her in the helicopter for the fifteen-minute flight to the hospital's trauma unit.

As the helicopter lifted off, the officer raced to her parent's house. He needed to be the one to tell them about the accident and drive them to the hospital. He knew how terrible it would be for them. She was their only daughter. As a doctor, her father would truly know how severe his daughter's injuries were. His plan was to call his wife and have her meet them at the hospital. They would stay with them and support them the best they could. He called dispatch, explained the situation, and raced to their house.

Trina had awakened three weeks later. She was unable to speak. They had removed the tube the week before. She could hear and understand what everyone was saying, but could not make them hear her. Her brain was working the way it would if she'd had a stroke. Her parents saw her eyes open and quickly got the nurse. They tried to convince the nurse that their daughter was awake. The nurse told them not to get their hopes up. Many comatose patients open their eyes and were not really aware of anything. She had heard the nurse, and understood exactly what she had said. She wanted to scream at them, 'I'm here!' She lay there for three days drifting in and out of consciousness. Twice a day they came in and removed the bandages covering the lower half of her body. She felt the pain as they scrubbed her down. The smell was revolting. She was not quite sure what the smell was. However, she would never forget it. It was the smell of something rotten. She silently begged God, 'please let me die'. Her Aunt Jeannie, a nurse at another hospital, came to visit her. She noticed Trina wrinkling her nose. She inspected Trina, then talked to her as if she was able to answer her back at any moment.

"Good morning Trina. I see they've been in and changed your bandages." She knew that Trina was unable to speak. Sometimes it took awhile for the voice to return after a tracheotomy. However, she'd seen her chart and knew that there had been some brain swelling. There was always the possibility that there had been some brain damage. Once again, she noticed Trina wrinkle up her nose. She heard a slight sniff.

"Trina do you she smell something?" Trina wrinkled up her nose again in reply. As Trina lay there, her aunt began to truly look at her.

"I can't believe they haven't done something with your hair. They have cleaned your burns, set your broken bones, but they couldn't clean the blood out of your hair?" She left the room and came back with some scissors, a pan of water, some shampoo, and a towel. "I know how much you love your long hair, but it is full of dried blood. I can only do so much to get rid of the blood and the smell. I know you smell the stench because you keep wrinkling your nose. I also know you hear me because you keep tracking me with your eyes. I knew you were awake." Her aunt made quick work of her hair. She cut it very short, washed and dried it, then gave her a sponge bath. Overall, she was in good condition. Her right leg was broken. She had to have her spleen removed because it had ruptured in the accident, when the car fell on her. The worst things about her injuries were the burns on her abdomen and legs. She had suffered second and third degree burns from just above her ankles to below the belly button. She would heal physically. However, mentally, healing would take a long time.

Lucas had heard that Trina was out of the coma and had come to visit her. He had been to her room several times. He had seen the damage that he had caused, and it made him sick. He had never had an alcoholic drink in his life, until that night. He had lied to his friends just to fit in. He did not even like the flavor of beer. How could he have known that one beer would have that kind of effect on him? He had asked the nurses daily if Trina was awake. His father had come one time and looked in on Trina. He told his son that he did not want him to hang out around Trina's room anymore, and he would not say why.

Lucas had asked his mom, on one of her visits, to find out if Trina would be okay. He did not even know how bad she was hurt. No one had told him anything. He later found out his father had told the hospital staff they were to give his son no information about Trina. Lucas' mother was the one who had told him that Trina had a broken right leg that would heal. She also told him that Trina had lost a lot of blood, and had died three times in the helicopter before they could get her stabilized. His mother had told him all of this before his father had walked in. She shut up the minute he entered the room. He asked if his son wanted anything while he went to get some coffee. Lucas told him that it would be great if his dad would bring him a soda. As soon as his father walked out of the room, his mother continued. She told him about Trina's burns. She watched the tears form in her son's eyes and continued. Trina would have at least a year of surgery, skin grafts and rehab to go through. She was going to need a lot of support. She would need to know that she still mattered to him, no matter how she looked. What his mother said shocked him. Of course he still cared about her. It did not matter what she looked like on the outside. She was a beautiful person on the inside. His father had overheard the conversation between Lucas and his mother. He sent his wife from the room and shut the door.

"Lucas, you have to understand how it would look if you kept dating Trina. She's going to be in here for quite some time. She's a sweet girl and all but what do you expect to happen when she gets out. You can't have her on the yacht. What would people think when they saw her horrible scars. She won't be invited to the country club looking like that."

"I don't care what the people at the country club might think. I just won't go to the country club any more. Besides, it was my fault that Trina was injured. After all, I'd been drinking and caused the accident."

"There will be no charges filed against you. We've found the motorcyclist who really caused the accident. The firm is going to handle the trial. We've worked out a deal with the motorcyclist. He'll plead guilty and lose his license for six months."

Lucas could not believe what his dad was saying. He had over reacted when he had seen the motorcyclist. The accident was his fault. In a stern voice, his father told him to drop the subject.

Three days later, his dad had come to take him home. When he arrived, Lucas was not in his room. Lucas had gone down to Trina's room with his best friend Mike. As they looked in the room, they thought she was sleeping. Her eyes were closed as her bandages were being changed. He had been told that she was heavily medicated. However, she still heard the conversation that took place outside of her room. She could hear two men talking. Someone was talking about how she would need a lot of support and care. It sounded like Lucas' best friend Mike. Because of the medication, she drifted in and out, only hearing bits and pieces. She did not recognize the third voice she heard. Suddenly she heard Lucas. He was saying that there was no way he could continue to date a hideous monster. He deserved only the best. After all, he was the captain of the soccer team. It was bad enough he was unable to participate in sports for the rest of the year. Surely, people didn't expect him to be seen with such a hideously scarred girl, only the best for him! Trina was horrified at what she had heard. Lucas turned toward Mike, and then told his father that he would be riding home with his friend. As Mike left the doorway, he saw a tear slide down Trina's face. He was afraid she had overheard the argument between Lucas and his father. He was also afraid that she had misunderstood what she had heard. Not permitted in her room while her bandages were changed, he never got the chance to confirm or deny any of it. She had heard enough to decide that she hated Lucas James and would never forgive him.

Trina shook the terrible memories from her mind. She would not be a victim again. She grabbed her aunt's hand and helped her stand up. She started to move toward the stairs. Her aunt was not moving. She seemed frozen in place. Trina looked at her and realized she was bleeding, and looked very disoriented. She grabbed her aunt's scarf from around her neck and tied it around her head to try to stop the blood from flowing. Once

51

again, they headed for the stairs. As she opened the door, she could see how smoky it was. She carefully stepped into the stairwell. She was unsure what had happened. She knew only one thing; she had to get out of the building. This was not going to be easy. Her aunt was very confused. There were already several people in the stairway from the floors above her. She thought about Mark and hoped that whatever had happened, he was safe. She stepped back inside the lobby for a minute. She pulled out her cell phone and tried to call Lucas. She wanted him to know that she was safe. She could not get a signal. She wondered if Mark had a cell phone. She wished she had asked, in case she had needed to ask him something. Now she had no way of contacting him or Lucas. She grabbed her aunt's hand and guided her into the stairway to join the others going down.

# 8 Shaken

Lucas was in the elevator of the South Tower on his way up to the sixty-fifth floor. He had heard a thump and thought to himself that they needed to check out the elevator or fix it. When he stepped off the elevator there seemed to be a lot of confusion. The phones were ringing, and there was a horde of people trying to get on the elevator. They shoved him aside. He walked to his father's office to find out what was going on, but no one seemed to know. They said smoke was pouring from the North Tower. They assumed there had been some sort of gas leak or something that had caused an explosion, possibly on one of the mechanical floors. Some people speculated that a small private plane may have veered off course and flown into the tower. They had heard that it was a plane. They had called downstairs and were told they were in no danger and that they needed to stay put. Lucas felt ill. Mark and Trina were in that building. He tried to call Trina on her cell. She either did not, or could not answer it. He went back into the office to find out where his father was. Mr. Sackett informed him that his father had an early court hearing. He did not expect it to last long and therefore, expected Lucas' father in around nine-thirty or ten. Lucas knew it would be useless to try to contact him. He would not even look at the phone if he were in court. He tried to reach Trina again. He wished that he had gotten Mark's number. Then again, he was not even sure if Mark had a cell phone.

He decided to go ahead and talk with Mr. Sackett about the benefit. The least he could do to help Trina now was what he had come here for. He explained to Mr. Sackett about the benefit. Like his father, Mr. Sackett wanted to know what big named people were on the list to attend the function. Unfortunately, that is how most of the people in his father's firm and country club felt. They wanted to know what big names were attending, how it would make them look to others, and would their name possibly be mentioned in the paper. Known as status, most of them looked good, smelled good, and were broke. They lived well above their financial means. It would not take much to wipe them out financially. Lucas did the best he could to remember some of the other names on the list, reciting them to Mr. Sackett. Mr. Sackett seemed impressed and pulled out his checkbook. Lucas told him all he needed at this time was to have him fill out a simple form. The money would be collected at the end of the week by the charity. In this way, the students of Eagle Prep would not be handling any of the funds.

Lucas checked his watch and realized it was nine o'clock. If his father's hearing was over, he should be able to reach him now. He stood up and excused himself. He figured he would try some of the other offices. He noticed several people staring out the windows toward the North Tower. Lucas ventured over for a look and was horrified at what he saw. Flames and smoke were billowing out. Imprinted on his brain for all eternity was the sight of people jumping. What could be so terrible that they would jump to their deaths? Were Trina and Mark in that mess, or were they safe. He noticed people with their cell phones out frantically trying to reach people they knew in the other tower. They seemed to be having trouble with the phones. Several people that Lucas had seen rushing into the elevator as he got off had returned to the floor. He overheard them talking. They had made it all the way down to the lobby, and then they were instructed to go back up. A few people decided instead to leave and go home. They were told that everyone and everything in their building was safe. One of the men in the crowd had received a call from a friend who was running late for work. Their friend had described the scene of chaos from the street. He told him that a plane had hit the North Tower.

Lucas stepped away from the crowd and tried to call Trina again. He was still unable to get through to her. He prayed that it was a problem just with her phone and that she and Mark were safe. Prayed, now that was a funny thought. The last time he had been to church was at Easter. The only time he could remember truly praying was after the accident when he thought he might go to jail. He realized he had deserved to go to jail. He also understood that had it not been for the father he almost despised, he would have gone to jail. It was not that his father did not think he deserved punishment. It was the idea that his father was concerned about what people would think if his son had gone to jail. That is why the motorcyclist had lost his license. Mr. Sackett was the attorney that had represented him. Obviously, his father could not because it would have been a conflict of interest. He had made it seem like the motorcyclist had recklessly pulled out at the last minute causing the accident. It helped their case when they traced the person down and, found he had had a previous record for drug possession. He just happened to be smoking some marijuana at the time they had showed up to interview him. When they threatened to call the police and have him arrested, he caved in. He admitted on the recording that he saw Lucas' car and thought he could beat it. He pulled out not realizing he had caused the accident. He took a plea bargain that involved community service and the loss of his license for six months. Lucas could not believe that his father had enough pull that he could make someone lie, just to save his sorry butt. Lucas had thanked Mr. Sackett, as his father had told him to, while his stomach churned. He was off the hook. He should have felt great.

The guilt he felt continued to nag at him until every time he saw his father the bitterness within him grew. Lucas doubted that his father truly loved him. After all, when he was a child visiting his grandmother he had taken some money from her purse for an ice cream. When she found out, she had spanked him. He remembered he had screamed at her that she didn't love him. She looked at him, hugged him close to her and said, "Oh baby boy, that is exactly why I spanked you. People who do not discipline their children probably don't really love them. I want you to know that I love you enough to discipline you."

This was one reason Lucas felt his father did not love him. He had never disciplined him. At least not that he could remember. If he and a friend got into a fight, it was always the other kid's fault, even if he had started it. He was always bailing him out of problems big or small.

Lucas headed down the hallway to the law offices of Traynor and Traynor. As he stepped inside the receptionist area, there was a loud explosion. Suddenly the whole building seemed to twist, tilt and sway at the same time. He thought the building was going to fall over. A wicked vibration went through the whole building. Tiles and light fixtures began to fall from the ceiling knocking Lucas to the floor, which seemed to drop a foot. The walls were torn, and jagged lines swept across them where once there had been smooth drywall. In some places, the drywall had completely popped loose from the wall. The air conditioning ducts popped out on top of them. The lights began to flicker, then went out. Just as quickly, as the lights had gone out they came back on. Lucas stood up and looked at the receptionist. Her phones started ringing. She answered them as quickly as possible letting the callers know that she did not know what had occurred.

Lucas cautiously stepped back into the hallway. Doors partially or completely popped out of their frames, hung at weird angles. The room filled with a chalky, white dust. There were small fires everywhere. It resembled a war zone. Lucas stood paralyzed with fear. He knew he needed to move and get out of there. Eyes wide, he jumped, startled by the sudden ringing of his phone. The voice on the other end was his mother's and she sounded extremely stressed. She wanted to know if he was with Trina and their friend Mark.

"How did you know Trina was involved in this charity fundraiser?"

"I called her mother the other day after you called me for advice about joining her in the fundraiser. I wanted to make sure everything would be okay with the two of you teaming up for this event. She assured me it was fine and told me that they still care for you. I figure what your father doesn't know won't hurt him."

"I totally forgot I had told you that Trina was involved."

"I've been watching the news about the airliner hitting the North Tower."

Lucas stopped her. He could hear the worry in her voice. "An airplane hit Tower One." We were told a plane hit it and I thought it was just a small private plane."

"No, it was a Boeing 767. I knew you were meeting Trina and Mark at the Trade Center for your fundraiser so I thought I'd check on you. I am so glad to hear you're not in the North Tower. I called your father and he had just gotten out of court. I told him what I'd seen. Since they had blocked off lower Manhattan, and he couldn't get to his office, he was heading home. I think you need to forget about the fundraiser and you and your friends need to head on home as well."

Lucas interrupted his mother. "Mom, Trina and Mark are in the North Tower. I've been trying to reach Trina but haven't been able to get through. I don't know if they were on the floor that's on fire or not. I saw smoke and flames coming out of the building. If I give you her number, will you please keep trying to reach her? Call me back please. I have to know they're okay. Listen mom, I have to go, they're telling us we have to evacuate now."

"Evacuate? Lucas, where are you", his mother asked as panic began to set in.

"I'm in the South Tower on the sixty-fifth floor. Our whole building just twisted and shook. The building was popping, cracking, and making horrible noises. The ceiling tiles and light fixtures started falling. Have you heard or seen anything else?"

His mother shoved her fist into her mouth and willed herself to calm down before she spoke to him. "Lucas, you have to get out now. I watched a second plane fly into your tower. The plane hit your building lower than the North Tower. They're saying it's a terrorist attack. Oh my gosh! People are falling or jumping from your building. Please Lucas get out now"!

Lucas did not need prodding. He ran to Mr. Sackett's office screaming for him. "Quick, we need to get out of here. A jet hit both towers and we need to leave now!"

"Go ahead Lucas, I'll catch up. I have some important papers and files I need to get." "Please", Lucas pleaded with him, "there's nothing here more valuable than your life."

"No, no, you go ahead, I need to take certain files with me. I'm sure I'll have plenty of time to leave the building. The firefighters will probably have the fire out before I need to leave. If not I'll be right behind you."

Lucas headed for the stairway, sadly leaving his father's law partner behind. He hoped he would make it out okay. Lucas knew not to take the elevators. He had always been told to take the stairs in case of a fire. There was a strong odor of smoke. He opened the door to the stairway only to find debris that had fallen from above, blocking it. He figured that must have been where the impact was. He followed others as they raced across the building to stairway A. He found so many people heading down. It was getting hard to breathe. The smoke was thick here, and there was debris everywhere.

He stepped into the stairway and closed the door behind him. He knew there was no turning back. Each stairway door locked from the inside, a security measure. To go back up he would have to go down about four floors to reach a door that would go back into the building. He thought back to that morning when he had stepped out of the mall and up to the security desk. He'd had to sign in and show identification so that he could go up to his father's office. He'd had to show the security guards his letter for the fundraiser so that they knew he would be visiting other offices on the floor. He thought it funny that they would have so much security for a building this tall. Now he wondered why it mattered. Not all the security in the world would have prevented what had just happened. He wondered if Mark and

Trina were having these same thoughts. Lucas reached the sixtieth floor. Suddenly there was a group of people going up.

"Where are you going?" he asked.

"Up because there is so much smoke below. That has to mean that there's a lot of fire below us."

"I just came from above. There are fires on the sixty-fifth floor so you should turn around and go back down."

They looked at him as if he was too young to understand anything in life. Lucas knew they were putting their lives in danger. He knew it would be just like talking to Mr. Sackett again so he closed his mouth, lowered his head in defeat, and continued down. He said a silent prayer for these people as they walked toward danger. It was funny that he now found himself praying consistently. He knew the Lord. He had not reached out to him in a long time. Maybe this is what it took for God to bring a rebellious teen back to him. He prayed for the strength to reach the ground level and the peace he needed not to panic.

As he reached the forty-fifth floor, the stairway door opened. Someone stepped into the stairway. Quickly he grabbed the door and stepped inside. He tried once again to reach Trina. After the third ring, she answered.

"Trina. Oh my gosh where are you?"

"I am in the stairway of the North Tower, around the fifty-third floor. I don't know where Mark is. I was hoping I'd find him in the stairway."

The stairway door opened and Trina quickly stepped inside. It looked like all of the rest of the offices with little cubicles everywhere.

"Lucas, it was terrible. My aunt was hurt and two men volunteered to help carry her down the rest of the way. Between the two of them, they felt they could get her some medical attention quicker. Something bad has happened to the building." Lucas could hear her begin to cry as she continued talking. "Fire came out of the elevator and burned people. I saw the windows blow out and people sucked out. A computer fell off the desk and hit my aunt in the head. When we stood up, we could hardly breathe because the air was so hot. I tied a scarf around my aunt's head and pulled my jacket over my mouth and headed for the stairway."

"Are you hurt Trina?"

"I'm fine. When the men asked to take my aunt down I assured her that I'd be just fine, and that I was sure that Mark was on his way down, and we would meet up. Lucas, I'm so scared. I don't know what happened. There was just some big explosion and the whole building shook."

"Trina, my mom called me just a little while ago. She said two airliners were hijacked and flown into both towers. I'm going to hang up now because we both need to get out. I'll meet you at Trinity Church on Liberty Street. If you get there before me just wait. Be safe Trina. I'll be praying for all of us."

Lucas hung up, opened the door and stepped back into the stairway. There seemed to be fewer people. He noticed water pouring down the stairs. The water appeared to be coming from broken water pipes above them. At least the air was clearer. He hoped it remained that way the rest of the way down. He made steady time going down the stairs. The silence gave his mind time to wander. What if he had decided not to join Trina in this fundraiser? Could he ever forgive himself if something happened to her? Would he have renewed his relationship with God? He hated the thought that he was one of those people who waited until something catastrophic happened to call on God. The stairway was eerily quiet for quite some time. As he exited the stairway onto the second floor, he could not believe his eyes. There was a gray dust hanging in the air. The stillness was unnerving. He looked at his watch. It had taken him forty-eight minutes to make it this far. He moved out into the deserted Plaza.

The area looked surreal. It was almost as if he had stepped onto a movie set. It was quiet, and there were multiple inches of dust everywhere. It almost resembled the dusty surface of a deserted planet. The whitish gray dust hung thick in the air making it hard to breathe.    The windows were gone, the glass had all been blown out. An officer directed him to a set of non-working escalators.    He had to walk down them, and then he went through a set of revolving doors and into the mall.  Told to exit by the Sam Goody's store, he followed the directions and all of the other people. Minutes later he stepped out into fresh air.

# 9 The Descent

Mark, Mr. Morrow and his secretary Margie made steady progress down the stairs. At times people turned around and headed back up the stairs to wait for rescue. They said it was too far to walk, they were too tired, and they had heard that the firefighters were on their way up. On several floors, they had to wait while someone came into the stairway with someone in a chair. They refused to leave people behind because they were elderly or disabled. At other times, they saw people on these floors refusing to leave because they had been instructed to wait for help.

Mark, surprised by how calm everyone was, continued down the stairs. There was not a lot of crying or anything. He figured in a situation like this there would be mass panic, people running and screaming down the stairs. He saw none of that. Occasionally they would need to move over as someone brought an injured person down. One woman appeared burned so badly, that her skin was bubbled, and in some places blackened and sagging. Her face, neck and arms seemed to have been injured the worst with her hair singed and her eyebrows gone. He was amazed she did not cry out in pain. She seemed to be beyond pain, and was in shock. She was lead silently down the steps in hope of finding medical help in time.

Time seemed to move in slow motion. They had moved quickly at first and seemed to be making good time. When the injured started to enter from different areas things slowed down. He knew that he was somewhere near the fifty-third floor. He slowed down when he saw a door to his right open. He stopped out of courtesy to let the person step into the stairway. Trina stepped out and turned around to thank the person who had let her enter. She had tried for several minutes only to have people refuse to slow down enough to let her slip into the stairway. She had to thank this person who had been so kind. She came face to face with Mark. She grabbed him and hugged him.

"Oh Mark, it's terrible! Lucas called me and said that terrorists flew planes into both of the towers. He wants us to meet him at Trinity Church on Liberty Street."

Mark did not say anything at first. When he finally got his voice, he told her what he had seen. "I know about the plane Trina, I was sitting in Mr. Morrow's office when I saw the plane coming straight for us. All I know for sure is that the plane hit somewhere above the office we were in. I don't know how high up, but I know that there was a lot of fire."

Trina told him of her experience and how her aunt was injured. "The worst part was seeing all of those people burning. Hearing the screams brought back memories of my accident."

The man behind them tapped Mark on the shoulder. "Excuse me young man. Did you say a plane flew into the towers?"

"Yes sir, I saw it with my own eyes. It was a big passenger jet. Trina just told me that a friend in the other tower said terrorists had flown planes into both towers."

Mark saw the terror and despair in the old man's eyes. "My wife works in the other tower. She called to tell me she was running real late. I sure hope she hadn't made it into work yet." Mark could only nod his head in acknowledgement.

As they walked down the stairs, Trina told Mark the complete story of her accident or at least the parts she remembered. She told him about the months she had spent in the rehabilitation center. She talked and talked to keep her mind off the immediate situation.

"When I woke up I could smell such a foul odor. The nurses came in each day and removed the bandages, from my waist down to my ankles. They had to be very careful because my right leg was broken. They couldn't put a cast on it because of the burns. I could see where they had sliced the skin open to help with the swelling. When you get a burn, fluid rushes to the area. To prevent the loss of fluid they put bandages on the burns. If too much fluid gathers then you run the risk of the skin bursting open. Therefore, they make slits in the skin to relieve the pressure. That wasn't the worst part. The worst part was that twice a day they had to come in, take the bandages off, and scrape off the dead skin. In the beginning, some of the skin was white and charred. In some areas, the skin looked like the outside of a marshmallow that had been burned black.

It looked like they could just pull it off. They would place me in a tub of water that would loosen the dead skin then scrub and scrape or pull it off. I cried, I screamed, and sometimes wished I would die. One day I said no more pity party for myself. "

"How long did it take your body to heal?"

"It took a long time. I had to wear a pressure garment for about a year to help the scars heal. It helped the raised, thick scars slowly go down. I developed contracture scars. The skin began to permanently tighten. That is when my hidden angel arrived, and he was a cute one at that. His name was Randy and he was my physical therapist. With contracture scars, the skin begins to contract and restricts movement. Some people have them so bad that they have to have surgery. I didn't need surgery, just lots of painful therapy. I asked Randy how long before I would be better. He told me if I worked hard and did everything he told me to do, that in three or four months I would be better. I decided to listen to him. "

"Did you have anyone else helping you?"

"I did. The reason I picked Angel Hope for our charity fund raiser, is because of what they did for me. They sent teens in to talk with me. Some of them had never experienced the pain of burns. They just wanted us to know that there were people like them that cared about people like me. That helped a lot because it seemed like most of my friends had deserted me. I don't blame them. I looked horrible and couldn't do the things they were doing. My new friends would walk me around the hospital and tell me jokes or we'd talk about the latest music. I still keep in touch with some of them. We go shopping and do things together. My best friend since the accident has been a girl named Alyssa. She had been a patient there from the time that she was three years old. She had suffered burns over a large part of her body and had to come in every so often for more surgeries. She is now getting ready for the last few plastic surgeries that will make her look as normal as possible. She was my coach. She and Randy would push me to walk up and down the stairs just one more time. When I was on my emotional roller coaster, she'd let me know it was okay. Some days I would laugh and some days, I would cry. They taught me to use the anger I felt, and I had a lot of it, when I was doing my therapy. It seems like I pushed myself harder on the days when I was angry."

"I think if I hadn't met Randy and Alyssa I would have given up on myself. When you suffer a burn, you lose a part of yourself. Not just physically lose yourself; you lose part of your identity. You have to decide who you really were and who you're going to be from that point on. You take time to grieve and then you move on with your life. It's not easy. I still have my days. I'll have those kinds of days for the rest of my life. However, I have chosen to face my fears and challenges head on and I'll never be a victim again. I am, and always will be a survivor."

Mark was quiet for quite some time. "I know what you mean about being a survivor. Sometimes it's hard being the only survivor. I told you my parents died in a house fire. What I didn't tell you was that it was my fault. My dad had bought me another model airplane to put together. From the time that I was small, he'd bought me model airplanes and cars. In the beginning, they were the simple snap together kind. He'd sit with me and show me how to snap the tiny pieces together, and how to read the directions. As I got older, they were more complicated. They became the kind that you glue together." Trina watched a smile play across Marks face as he remembered the good times.

"My parents felt it was important to do things together as a family. It was especially important after they both lost their hearing. My mother lost her hearing gradually. She had a disease that affected her inner ear. My father lost his hearing in an explosion. They thought it was important to maintain a normal life. That was one of the reasons they continued to buy me the models. The only thing that they did different was had a special type of smoke alarm wired into the house. In case of a fire, the alarm would go off and lights would blink on and off so that they could get out. They couldn't hear the alarm, but they could feel the vibrations from it."

"The night of the fire, I'd been working on a really cool plane model. I'd put some glue onto a piece of paper to make it easier to use. I used a toothpick to place the glue on the part. I hated the smell of the glue, so I opened a window and lit a stick of incense, something I always did. While the part was drying, I sat on my bed with my headphones on, and read the next set of directions. I guess I was tired, and I fell asleep. There was a cool breeze blowing into the room. It blew the incense out of its holder. Since the glue was very flammable, the incense ignited the paper. The next thing I knew I was choking. I woke up and saw my room engulfed in flames. I couldn't get to the door, it was blocked. There were so many flames, and it was so hot in the room. I climbed out of the window. I ran around to the front of the house and tried to get in. I could see the flames shooting through the roof. A neighbor tried to get into the house to my parents. It was just too hot. I should have been able to save them. I should have died in that fire instead of them. It was my fault that they died. I killed them."

"Mark, you had nothing to do with their death. It was an accident. You didn't cause the breeze to come through the window and knock the incense out of its holder."

"If I hadn't been working on that stupid model, the fire would never have happened.

"You're right. There might have been a gas leak or an explosion. The fire could have started in their room by a short of some type. You are not God. You did nothing wrong. It's time that you stop being a victim, and you need to realize that it's okay to be a survivor. You're experiencing what they call survivor's guilt. Many people experience it during a catastrophe when they're the only one left alive. You have to realize it's okay to be that survivor."

On the forty-fourth floor Trina and Mark switched to a different stairway. This was where they began to see the firefighters. They were encouraged to continue down the stairs. The firefighters and police officers looked totally worn out. Some of them paused to catch their breath. They continued in silence down the stairs as the brave firefighters continued up. The firefighters reminded them to be careful; the stairway was slippery with a mixture of jet fuel and water. As they reached the thirtieth floor, they felt a rumbling that shook them. It was difficult to stand upright in the stairway. People began to scream and panic in fear. The rumbling lasted only a few seconds and then everything was silent again. The procession down the stairs continued. People seemed to hurry a little more quickly since hearing the rumbling, fearing another plane had flown into the building.

Suddenly a smell reached their noses. Someone suggested that it was burning jet fuel. There seemed to be more smoke here than above. They wondered why there was so much smoke if the fires were above them. Had something happened to create fires below? Were they going to be trapped in the stairway? These were the questions going up and down the stairs.

More firefighters began to come up the stairs. They carried their tanks on their backs, huge masks, and a large roll of hose over their shoulders. They assured everyone that it was safe to continue down the stairs. The heat was worse the further down they went. This made no sense. Everyone wondered why it was so hot, even though the firefighters assured them there was no fire below. Many people began to take off their jackets and leave them in the stairs. For once, Trina was happy that she had worn her flats. She saw several pairs of high heels lying in the stairway. They were becoming a hazard to those walking down the stairs. Trina knew that had she chosen the heels that morning that her shoes would have joined the many pairs over which she had to step. The firefighters told them to cover their faces with whatever they had, to make it easier to breathe. They hadn't heard the fire alarms going off until they reached this level. Maybe it was because they had been talking about other things, focused on getting down and out. The narrow stairway made it impossible to not hear them now. The alarms echoed loud and clear.

Mark looked at the door to his right. It said they were on the eighteenth floor. Suddenly they were ankle deep in water. He noticed water beginning to cascade down the stairs like a series of waterfalls. The stairs became slippery. He looked up and noticed that the water was coming from broken water pipes above them. They continued steadily down. As they reached the ninth floor, there was more water. Mark and Trina could see that the smoke was thicker and the water that rained down on them smelled as if it were mixed with jet fuel. Trina began to panic. She thought to herself, what if something ignited the jet fuel in the water. Would it burn? Mark noticed the panicked look in her eyes and knew what she was thinking. He tried to calm her.

"Take a deep breath and calm down." Everything is going to be okay. They told us there is no fire down here and I believe them."

Silently Trina began to pray. She knew that she could trust God to take care of her no matter what. That thought and her prayers began to calm her fears. She felt a peace that seemed unnatural and knew that it was God covering her fears. Mark noticed the peaceful look on her face and looked at her quizzically.

"I prayed for us. I prayed for safety and peace to calm our fears."

Mark smiled at her. He had not thought about prayer. He was sure God would not listen to him after the terrible thing he had done. He had gotten his parents killed. However, for some unexplained reason he felt peaceful. He knew that things would be all right. He could always talk with Trina about her beliefs later if he wanted to.

Quickly they emerged onto the second floor. The room was full of diffused light, as dust and smoke whirled around them. Where had it all come from? They paused only a moment to look around. Someone was shouting at them to run and leave their shoes on. Trina looked down and for the first time saw all of the glass on the floor. It was then that Trina and Mark realized that all of the windows had been blown out. There was glass inside as well as outside of the building. Trina thought about all of the shoes she had seen in the stairway. She felt sorry for the women who had left them behind. She realized the pain and agony that they must have endured running through the broken shards. She saw the floor smeared with blood. Strangely, there seemed to be more blood on the floor than what there should have been from women cutting their feet on the glass. Where had it all come from? A strong feeling of panic filled the air around them. Some of the people with them began to scream and cry again.

Another officer stepped forward and directed them down a broken escalator covered with water. It was difficult to keep their footing on the slippery steps, but they went as quickly as possible. Water ran through the mall making the floors slippery. In front of them was a set of revolving doors, even they had not been spared. Heavy glass crunched under their feet as they ran through them. They ran following everyone else toward Borders Bookstore, as the officers had instructed them. Ahead of them loomed another non-working escalator. They ran up the steps as quickly as they could. Every lift of their leg to the next step felt like an added ten pounds of weight. The officers directing them seemed to have a tone of urgency in their voice that bordered on panic, yet they appeared to be calm. Maybe it was an act to keep the others from panicking, or maybe it was just a part of their job. Trina suddenly felt comforted knowing there was someone in authority telling everyone what to do. If there had not been someone there directing everyone, it would have been a scene of total chaos. Besides, the firefighters were on their way up and would surely be able to get the fire under control. This building had stood the test of time. It was a symbol of strength.

Trina and Mark made their way to the courtyard where on a normal day they could find the German Sculpture "The Sphere." This sculpture had sat in the center of a ring of fountains for many years. However, this was not a normal day. Trina and Mark paused and looked around. Their surroundings resembled a scene in a movie where a nuclear bomb had gone off, and the area was full of fallout. They knew this had been no nuclear blast, and it was definitely not a scene from a movie. There had to be at least five inches of gray, pasty, soot on the ground, and swirling lazily through the air. Everywhere they looked, they could see twisted steel and wire. There were chunks of concrete steel protruding at all angles. As they viewed the scene, they realized debris was still falling. As it landed near them, they noticed some of it was still on fire and some of it was smoldering. Trina recognized parts of an airplane. It brought the phone call she had received from Lucas into focus causing her to suddenly gasp. She finally realized what he had actually been trying to explain to her. There had been a small part of her sure that Lucas' mother had been mistaken about the airliner. Here was the indisputable proof.

The next thing Trina saw made her turn and bury her face in Mark's shoulder. There were bodies and body parts everywhere. She wished she could erase these pictures from her mind. Mark held her as they walked as quickly as they could, while trying to navigate the debris. He knew that this would haunt them both, for the rest of their lives. They exited the building quickly through the doors. As they ran, they noticed the blood streaked street. At the same time, they continued to hear loud thumps around them. Mark heard a noise to his side and paused to investigate. It appeared to be a high-pitched whine. Trina stopped and looked up as well. Her hand flew to her mouth as she tried to stifle the scream that was coming from her. The whining noise stopped with a loud thud. Mark and Trina realized that the sound they had previously heard was the thud of bodies hitting the pavement. They turned their eyes forward and began to run again. They had only covered about a quarter of a block when they heard a thunderous rumble. The ground vibrated beneath their feet as they ran for their lives.

# 10  Stumble in the Dark

Lucas stepped outside and prepared to cross Liberty Street. He felt a rumbling, looked up and began to run. The tower he had just walked out of was coming down. He knew there was no way he could outrun the debris. His survival instinct took over. He ran as fast as he could. Suddenly propelled through the air, he landed hard on the ground with debris covering him. His body felt hot, as if he were burning. The terror took over as he began to claw his way to the top of the debris that pressed down on him, threatening to entomb him. Finally, his arm broke through. He pushed away the remaining debris and stood up. Realizing his jacket was indeed on fire he quickly removed it and tried to run. He could not see. Everything was suddenly so dark and grey, leaving an ominous feel to the air. He stumbled around the debris trying to find a route to safety. He felt disoriented and confused. What had happened? He tried to remember. The last thing he remembered was a loud rumbling, running, and debris beginning to fall around him. He had slowed long enough to look behind him and realized the building he had just exited was falling. He did not take time to ponder what he should do, he just ran. A hot blast of debris had blown him down the street. Hesitantly he lifted his hand to the back of his head and realized the hair was singed off. He smacked at it to make sure there was no fire. He was scraped up pretty bad, but he was alive. Blood trickled down his face from a gash beside his eyebrow. When he tried to move he felt a throbbing pain in his right shoulder. It was hard to move it. It was becoming more difficult to breathe. Every breath he took was a painful realization that he was suffocating on the dust. He had to get it out of his mouth so he could breathe. He tried to take a breath to cough. What he sucked in was more dust and tiny pebbles.

Suddenly he heard a noise. Someone was calling for help. He tried to look around, but could see nothing. Lucas groped his way toward the noise. He coughed and tried to call out. "Where are you?" He listened in silence for what seemed like forever.

Maybe it had been his imagination. He heard the noise again. He walked toward what he thought was the street. It was impossible to see anything. Once again, he heard the cry, "Help, please don't leave me."

Unexpectedly a hand reached out of the dust, grasped at him as he began to pass, and succeeded in grabbing his pant leg. Lucas screamed and jumped in fright. He could just make out a gray, dust covered hand. An iron gate was lying on top of the body buried beneath.

"Hold on, I'll try to lift this gate off of you." Lucas took a deep breath and lifted the gate as high as he could, ignoring the pain in his shoulder. The body slowly crawled out. He lowered the gate to within a few inches of the pavement and let it fall. The young woman grasped his arm; pulling so hard, she almost toppled them both.

"You must be my guardian angel", she cried, as she hugged him, squishing what little air he had out of his lungs. He slowly pulled away from her and noticed a large gash on her leg. He removed his tie and wrapped it around the gash to try to stop the flow of blood. He began to nervously giggle as he looked at the tie. He hated ties and found this a better use for it. Continuing to cough, they stood up and looked around. There was nothing but rubble and dust everywhere. Together they stumbled down the street away from the disaster. The area looked like a war zone. They could see no one. Lucas had walked in heavy fog where you could not see your hand before your face. This was different. Not only could you not see what was in front of you, but you could still feel the debris in the air. Miniscule pieces of rocks, dust, paper, and other unidentifiable things were floating all around them, pricking at their skin. It was like being in a thick soup. They headed north up Liberty Street. Cassie began to cry. She kept mumbling to herself.

"I have to get home to Shasha." I have to make sure she's okay."

Lucas had passed Trinity Church by a half a block when he remembered he had asked Trina to wait for him there. He wanted to turn around and look for Trina. The young woman holding on to him had such a tight grip on him he knew that they would walk on. They stumbled into the nearest store, a block from where they had picked themselves up. As they entered, someone thrust a bottle of water into their hands. Lucas filled his mouth up with the cool liquid and tried to swallow. His mouth was so full of dust. All he could do was rinse his mouth out. The mud in his mouth created by the water had to be spit out before he could drink in the cool liquid. The owners led them to a table and told them to sit. He asked the young woman with him her name.

"Cassie, my name is Cassie. What's yours?"

"My name is Lucas. I can't believe what just happened. How could a plane bring down the tower?"

"What do you mean a plane? Who said a plane hit the tower?"

Lucas told her about the planes hitting the North and South Towers. He explained he had been on the phone with his mother right after the North Tower was struck. She had been explaining to him what had happened as she was watching it on the TV.

She had actually seen the plane hit the tower that I was in. She wanted to make sure I wasn't in Tower One. My friends are still in there. I know that at least one of them is okay. I'd been able to get through to her and she was on her way down. I don't know about my friend and classmate Mark. I know he was on the eighty-eighth floor. I was sitting in my father's law firm when the plane hit. I begged Mr. Sackett, my dad's partner, to leave with me. He was trying to get papers together. He told me to leave him. I don't think that he got out. I barely made it out. " He knew he was nervously rattling on.

Suddenly Lucas began to sob uncontrollably. If his father could see him now he'd probably be ashamed of him and call him weak for crying. He didn't care. He had held all of his feelings and fear inside of himself. He had managed to hold it together all the way down the stairs of the tower. He had been determined not to panic while still in the staircase. He had tried to act courageous. Now that he was out, he let all of his feelings erupt to the surface. Cassie hugged him and they cried together. Crying was good for the soul. He figured he would cry for many nights to come.

Cassie pulled away from him, cleared her throat and asked him what he was doing in the towers. He looked at her before he answered. He could tell she was trying hard to hold it together. He explained that he was a student at Eagle Prep. Part of his graduation requirements was community service. He and two of his friends were at the Trade Center that morning to finalize plans for a charity fundraiser dinner at Windows on the World. His ex-girlfriend was in charge of the fundraiser. She had been a burn victim and so Angel Hope had been her personal choice for a charity fundraiser. Once again, Lucas began to cry. Cassie sat patiently. She knew that this young man needed time to tell what was on his mind.

He told Cassie that the reason Trina had been in the burn center was an accident he had caused. After the accident, his father had made him break off their relationship. It was unfair to both of them. He had felt guilty for so long because he had never been able to tell her how sorry he was. He had hoped that by working with her on the charity she would give him a chance to apologize and try to make things right.

Cassie listened patiently. It took every ounce of strength she had to sit there. The streets were still so full of dust. It covered the inside of the store where they sat. They had to wait a while longer before they could leave. She needed to get out of there. She had to find her daughter. She knew if she lost it now that this young man who was with her would probably lose it as well. She watched this young man before her mature before her eyes. She let him know that by pulling her from under the gate that had pinned her to the ground, he had made good on making things right. She told him about her little girl Sasha. As she began to talk about Sasha who was only four years old she began to shake and cry. She needed her mommy because she'd lost her daddy in a warehouse fire the year before. Her husband had been a firefighter. Suddenly she gasped and began to sob, rocking back and forth on the chair.

"Oh my gosh, all those firefighters. They were still in the building when it fell."

It was Lucas' turn to comfort her. He knew the realization that the firefighters had probably never had a chance was something that brought her husband's death to the front of her mind. He knew how she felt. She felt helpless, empty, and full of guilt. He knew this because he felt the same way. Why was it that they had survived and others had not? Cassie stood up and headed for the door. Lucas began to follow. She stopped him and told him that she would be okay. She understood that he had told his friends that he would meet them somewhere. She hugged him and then looked him in the eye and told him that he needed to try to find them. She had friends that she could call to drive her to her daughter's daycare and then to the hospital to get her leg stitched up. She hugged him one more time and kissed him on the cheek. Then she thanked him sincerely for saving her life, so that she could go home to her daughter.

Lucas left her and headed back toward Trinity Church. He continued to choke on the dust that hung in the air. He could see officers setting up barricades. They were beginning to shut down the lower portion of Manhattan and they stopped him just a few blocks from his destination. He tried to explain to the officer that he needed to get to the church to meet his friends. They were in the North Tower. He was sure that since he was only a block away they would let him go to find his friends. Suddenly the ground began to shake violently, and Lucas heard the unmistakable sound he had heard such a short time before. Tower One was coming down. Thick, black smoke, ash and debris headed their way. He could see orange flames mixed in with the evil looking cloud. The only thing that came to his mind was that Satan was in control of this day and was making his Hell on earth. The officer grabbed him and they began to run. They could see others in front of them running. In the panic people were knocked to the ground. Some stopped to help them up, and in the process found themselves knocked down. Lucas suddenly found himself on the ground once again. People were stepping on him as they ran. His ribs ached from being trampled. He forced himself up. He knew if he did not stand, debris or people running would crush him. He stood and helped an elderly man who had fallen beside him, to his feet. His ribs ached and he was out of breath. He could no longer run so he walked as fast as he could, holding the arm of the elderly man he had assisted. His new mission, it seemed, was to get this stranger to safety. He looked so frail and fragile. Lucas didn't know if Trina and Mark had made it out. He could hear explosions coming from behind him. He figured it had to be cars exploding as debris dropped on them. His biggest concern now was whether he would be able to out-walk this second cloud of dust and debris. Deciding they would not be able to get out of its path, he pulled the man into an alcove of a nearby building. They flattened themselves against the building as the debris blew by. Lucas had positioned himself behind the older man shielding him from the majority of the debris. He could feel his shirt ripping as debris flew by. He felt a white hot pain shoot through his back as something hit him. The air was hotter this time, and had an acrid taste. He feared never being able to catch his breath again. The roar finally subsided and Lucas stepped from the alcove. Where were all of the people who had been behind him? When he had stood up to help the old man, there were people behind him in the distance running for their lives. He knew they should have caught up to him and the older man. Where were they? Suddenly he realized the unthinkable. The other people had not made it. Once again, he headed north, this time with a different person in tow.

At the end of the block, they saw a Snapple truck pull up. Someone was in the back handing out drinks to those passing by.

These people must have been angels in disguise. How could they have known that people would desperately need something to drink? He and the older man walked in silence down the street with their drinks. Neither of them said a word. Suddenly the man stopped.

"I can't go any farther."

He was holding and rubbing his chest with one hand while searching for something in his pocket with his other hand. Lucas helped him sit on the sidewalk.

"What is it you need? What are you looking for?"

"I have a bottle of nitroglycerin tablets I take for my heart. I came from the eighty-first floor of the North Tower and I didn't have a single chest pain until now. I think my body and mind are finally catching up with the events."

Lucas found a tiny bottle and opened it. "How many?"

"Just one, please put it under my tongue."

The man was too weak to even place the pill under his own tongue. Lucas sat beside the older man. They were both having difficulty breathing through the dust filled air, yet the man's labored breathing changed. Lucas knew that the change was not due to his heart problems; it was due to the dust. Lucas decided to sit with the man until he was able to stand and walk again. He did not want to leave him. What if something happened to him and no one was around. He did not think he could stand that kind of guilt.

The old man held out his hand.

"Ken Graham. I'm a lawyer with the firm of Graham and Sons. My sons were not here today, thank God. Their mother's in the hospital, and they were on their way to visit her. I was supposed to go to the office and gather up a few files they needed for a hearing tomorrow, and meet them at the hospital. I volunteered to go to the office because the stress of my wife being in the hospital has caused me to have some chest pains lately. They were afraid if I spent too much time there, I'd end up in a bed next to her. In light of what just happened, I'm glad that I was the one in the building and not my sons. I don't know if their mother and I could stand it if something this horrific had happened to them. I need to try to reach them at the hospital and let them know that I am okay."

Instinctively Lucas reached into his pocket for his phone. He remembered it flying from his hands when the first tower fell, and he was blown through the air. He would have gladly let the old man use his phone.

"I'm sorry but mine got lost in the first collapse."

"What first collapse?" the older man inquired.

"I was in the South Tower at my father's law firm when the second plane flew into my building. I was with my father's business partner and decided to evacuate. I reached the bottom and went out the door when I heard a loud rumble and the ground began to shake. I looked behind me and saw the building I'd just left collapsing. I made it just a few yards away from the building when I was blown down the street and covered in debris. I crawled out only to find my jacket on fire and my phone gone from my hand."

"Well, that explains the strange haircut. I just assumed it was some new fad", Ken joked.

Lucas began to laugh and then grabbed his side.

"What's wrong?"

"I think I may have some cracked ribs. As I was knocked down, several people ran right across me. That's how I came to find you. I guess I was meant to find you in the street."

"Well I sure am glad you did. I couldn't have gotten up by myself. My strength was all gone. When I got knocked down I just prayed, 'Lord send someone to help me or else make it quick and painless'. I felt a total peace. By the way, what am I supposed to call the angel that God sent to me in my time of need?

Lucas laughed. This was the second time in the last hour that he, had been called an angel. In his mind, he was definitely no angel. "My name's Lucas James. Trust me I am no angel. I was in the South Tower working on my community service hours."

"You got in trouble with the law and they sent you to the Trade Center to do community service?"

Lucas grabbed his ribs as he once again doubled over with laughter. He quickly straightened up. He felt the nauseating, white-hot pain in his back again. He thought that maybe he had pulled or torn some major muscles in his back. He assumed his back was bruised, and scraped from the blast and debris.

"I'm not in trouble with the law. I'm a student at Eagle Prep and we have to complete twenty-five hours of community service to graduate. I was in my father's law firm picking up the signed forms for our fundraiser, Angel Hope. We were supposed to be having a thousand dollars a plate dinner at Windows on the World this next week."

The old man began to laugh. " I'm familiar with the Angel Hope charity. That's one dinner I guess I'll no longer be attending. I'd filled out one of those forms. Some young woman had sent them to our offices. I filled one out because I had a nephew that was in the burn unit at age three. They visited him every day. They sat with him when he had to do his therapy. They distracted him from the pain. They helped him survive. Once everything settles, maybe we can still do the fundraiser somewhere else."

"Trina" Lucas choked out. Trina is the young woman who sent the forms to your office. She was in the North Tower along with Mark, a friend of ours. I was on my way back to see if I could find them when the building began to collapse. Some cop grabbed my arm and pulled me around. We started to run. I don't know what happened to him. I hope he made it. Then, I was knocked to the ground and found you."

"Young man, I'd love to thank you for helping me out. I probably would've died right there on that spot if you hadn't help me. If you hadn't helped me I wouldn't be able to see my wife and kids again."

Lucas had received several lessons this day on how precious life was. He didn't always like his father, but he wanted nothing more than to see the faces of his parents. He asked Ken if he was able to stand. When he nodded affirmative, he helped Ken to his feet while ignoring the pain in his back. Lucas took one look at the dust-covered man and realized he couldn't tell what race he was because of the dust. He began to giggle.

"What did I miss?" Ken asked.

"I was just thinking that I must be covered in twice the amount of dust that you're covered in. I was also thinking that no one today could judge anyone based on their race because we are all one color today, debris gray." He laughed again and Ken laughed with him. They headed north once again at a slow pace. Lucas was still worried about his friends, but as Ken had said, he just had to turn it over to God and let him handle it. He hoped his friends were alive somewhere. His job right now was getting Ken some place where they could find a phone to let his family know he was okay.

# 11 Televised Terror

Lucas' mother sat in her living room trying repeatedly to reach her son. She heard her husband pull into their drive. As he entered the house, he noticed the panicked look on his wife's face. She ran to him and grabbed him sobbing.

"What's wrong? I heard rumors on the ferry another plane hit the South Tower and one crashed into the Pentagon. How bad is it? What do you know? Is it Mr. Sackett?"

His wife stood staring at him and suddenly began to collapse. He grabbed her and sat her on the couch. Concerned, he went to get her a glass of water. Grasping the glass with trembling hands, she took a sip, sat the glass down and turned to him.

"I spoke with Lucas" she started to say.

"Good, he should be on his way home now", he said interrupting his wife.

She stared at him. "John, he was inside the South Tower when it was hit. He told me he was evacuating. Trina and Mark were in the North Tower."

"Why in heaven's name was he with Trina?"

"Did you hear what I said?" She screamed at him. "They were all in the Towers when they were hit. I've not been able to reach Lucas or Trina. I just watched both of the Towers collapse. What if they didn't get out?"

"What do you mean the Towers collapsed? There's no way those towers can be brought down by a couple of planes. I know you're upset but let's not get hysterical."

She looked at him with a look that bordered on contempt. She was not some hysterical woman, who took a situation and blew it out of proportion. She had never given him reason to think that she was being over-dramatic in what she said. She took him by the arm and led him into the living room where the television replayed the morning's events over, and over. She jabbed her finger in the direction of the television. He watched in horror as he saw for himself the planes fly into the Twin Towers.

He stared in disbelief as first one, and then the other tower collapsed.

"Why in heaven's name were they in the Towers?" He stopped, and answered his own question.

"Oh no, the fundraiser. They were there for the charity dinner fundraiser. I remember at breakfast this morning Lucas told me; he had to go to my office to collect the forms for the fundraiser. I was too busy bragging to my friends to pay attention to what he was saying. What time was he there? How do you know he was in the building when it was hit? Have you talked to him?"

His wife could hear the panic beginning to enter into his voice. She had never seen this side of him. He always seemed to be the calm one. He was always the one in control. She knew he was beginning to panic because this was something he could not control.

"I called Lucas when I saw the second plane fly into the South Tower. I thought that all of them had been in the North Tower because they had to set things up with the restaurant. He told me that he was evacuating because something had happened and that Trina and Mark had been in the North Tower when the plane had crashed into it. He didn't know if they were okay or not. I had briefly explained to him what I'd seen on the news.

"I tried calling Trina's cell phone but couldn't get through. The fundraiser was Trina's idea. Do you want to know why your son was there? Lucas has felt guilty about Trina's injuries ever since the accident. The problems that exist between you and your son are there because you let him off the hook. He felt that he deserved to be punished for the accident. He also knows that Trina overheard the argument the two of you had in the hospital, outside of her room. Mike told him that she looked right at him and was crying after your argument. That's why she hasn't spoken to him. She thought he didn't want to be with her because of the way she would look. She never knew it was you that didn't want her around. She never gave Lucas a chance to explain. He felt so guilty that he just took what she gave him and let it go. He felt that he deserved at least that much punishment. He'd hoped that by helping her with this fundraiser she would finally be able to forgive him. If that happened then maybe, he'd be able to forgive himself. My only hope was that it would allow him to forgive you, so that the two of you would be able to have some sort of a relationship. The direction he was headed in life, he would have graduated, and you probably would not have seen him again. His feelings were bordering on hatred toward you. You never let him make his own choices unless they agreed with yours. Did you know he wants to be a P.E. teacher and help sculpt the minds and bodies of other kids? Do you think he'd tell you that?" Her voice was bordering on hysterics again. "He loves you so very much, but told me he'd rather end up the poorest person on earth and do what he enjoys, than have all of your money and end up miserable. He thinks you're a fake. You were losing your only son, and didn't even know it. Now, you may have lost him and his friends forever."

Mrs. James began to cry uncontrollably. Her husband sat beside her and held her. She felt a tear hit her shoulder and realized her husband was crying. He had never thought about what his son actually wanted. It had always been his way or no way. When he thought about it, he had treated his own wife this same way. She was right; he had always worried about appearances. What other people thought about them would not bring his son home safe and sound. All he could do was pray that God would protect not only his son, but also Mark and Trina. He prayed that he would have the opportunity to get to know Mark and ask Trina to forgive him. He stood up, went to the phone, and called Trina's parents. No one answered.

# 12 Out of the Ashes

Trina and Mark heard the rumble from behind them. Mark ventured a glance behind them and what he saw sent shivers down his spine.

"Run", he screamed.

Trina looked over her shoulder as Mark grabbed her hand. The building they had just exited was coming down. The floors fell like dominoes crushing and pulverizing everything into dust and ashes. A boiling, black cloud of debris flowed toward them. The first thing that popped into Trina's mind was the pictures she had seen on television when Mount St. Helens blew up. The pyroclastic cloud that had rolled down that mountain had wiped out everything in its path. Trina knew they were in trouble. The heat coming from the cloud was beginning to burn her skin. This was a feeling she had felt before. She held Mark's hand tighter, screaming as she ran, and prayed for it to end quickly.

The cloud caught up to them before they had run ten steps. They stumbled over something in the street and went sprawling on the ground. Mark quickly rolled close to Trina, trying to cover her body with his. He prayed that their death would be quick. The flames and heat shot over his body scorching his skin. Suddenly he felt the blows of debris hitting his back. His one and only thought was to protect Trina. He would not let her burn again, even if it meant he did. He did not see himself as being a hero. If he protected her, maybe God would forgive him for killing his parents. The roar was deafening and then there was total silence. He wondered if he was dead. He tried to move and found it difficult. He knew if he did not extricate himself from the debris then he would not be able to help Trina. He put his hands on the ground and tried to raise himself up but found the task too difficult. He fell back to the ground, weighed down by whatever was on top of him. Tina was fine. She had rolled next to a car. The car and Mark had protected her. She stood up and began to pull things off the top of Mark. He was beginning to experience severe difficulty breathing. The choking, thick dust and the weight on him were too much. He felt himself beginning to black out. He could hear Trina's voice from far away.

"Don't you dare give up on me! Do you hear me? I said, you had better not give up on me! You will not be a victim! You will not leave me alone! You will survive! Talk to me! If you can do nothing else then say my name! Come on! Let me hear it. Trina, say Trina!"

Mark could feel the pressure beginning to let up. He was able to barely squeak out her name. Trina moved chunks of concrete and hot, twisted metal that covered Mark. She coughed violently every time she moved although she continued to make slow progress. It took her ten minutes to remove enough debris that Mark could help to pull himself free. Trina had looked around for someone to help her. Where were all of the people that had been running with them? Had they been so selfish that they had just run away and left those who needed help? She felt guilty for those thoughts. She knew that just like her they had been running for their life. They were only trying to survive.

Mark and Trina stood and looked around. All that was left of the Twin Towers were piles of burning and smoking rubble and twisted metal. No one would be able to tell which building was which. Trina noticed the back of Mark's shirt was gone. She also noticed his blistered back and neck. She needed to get him some medical help. She recognized the second degree burns. He had no hair on the back of his head. She decided not to say anything to him unless he mentioned it. She knew the pain would soon set in. His pants were shredded. She could see ugly bruises beginning to form. One leg seemed to be at a strange angle. She didn't know if it was broken or severely bruised.

"Mark, are you able to walk?"

"What? Walk? Where?"

Trina wasn't sure if he was in shock or just as confused as she was. "I don't know where we have to go but we can't stay here."

She took Mark's arm and began to lead him away. He winced with every step he took. He looked down at his leg and saw the funny shape of it. He knew it was probably broken. He decided immediately that if he could survive getting out of a burning building and its collapse then he would walk out of this disaster area somehow. His biggest priority right now was getting as far away from the swirling debris as he could. He was breathing in whatever was floating in the air. Suddenly he leaned over and vomited. It was the sudden realization that mixed in with the dust and bits of concrete that he and Trina breathed in, was probably pieces of pulverized bodies. As if to attest to this, he looked down between his shoes where he had just vomited and saw a small piece of bone by his left foot. It looked to be a finger with most of the tissue burned away. Mark vomited again.

"Are you okay?"

"Sure, I just had to get rid of all of the dust so that I could breathe." He knew the remark sounded lame, even to him but he didn't want to tell her what he had just figured out, or what he had seen at his feet. He looked up and took a good look at Trina. He wanted to make sure that she was okay. He saw the blood soaked shirt.

"Trina, are you okay? Your back is covered in blood. Are you cut? Did you get hurt when you fell?"

Trina looked at him. She wasn't hurt that she knew of. She asked him to lift the back of her shirt to check for injuries. He looked and realized that the blood was not hers. Trina started to cry, immediately realizing where the blood had come from. The blood of those who were behind them that had perished in the collapse of the building covered her. It was her turn to be sick. As she bent over, she saw something sticking out of her leg. It hurt, but she was afraid to look too closely, so she did her best to ignore it. There would be a time and place to have it checked out. She wiped her mouth as she stood up and told Mark that they needed to try to walk north.

Mark let Trina lead him slowly up West Broadway Street. He needed water. He needed to rinse the awful taste and debris from his mouth. He needed a doctor. He had to lean on Trina for every step. He would take one step and then drag his other leg. They made slow progress. He noticed the light was beginning to filter through the dust and he could begin to make out the voices and silhouettes of other people. He knew they would be okay. They walked past city hall and stopped at a small deli asking if anyone had any water. The water had all been given away. A man, probably the owner, begged them to come in so that he could get a pitcher of water to wash out their eyes. Trina led Mark into the store. She sat him on a chair. The owner's wife came out from a back room with a pitcher and a large bulb syringe. She poured some of the water into a large bowl, and using the syringe, she washed as much of the dust and debris from Mark's face as she could. She had him lean his head back. She asked Trina to hold his eyes open so that she could flush them out. She filled the syringe with water and gently squeezed the cool liquid into his eyes. She repeated the process until she could see no more debris. She knew she had not gotten it all, but she knew that it would be enough until he could get to a hospital. Mark could finally see clearly. He prepared to get up from the chair. The owner of the store told him to stay in the chair. He went to his shelves and returned with a package of white hand towels. He took a pair of scissors and cut strips from one towel. He took the scissors and cut the strips of shredded cloth from Mark's pants. He wrapped the towel tightly around the leg, and with his wife's help, he secured it with the strips of towel. He went into the back room again and returned with a clean shirt. He helped the young man removed his burned and shredded shirt. Mark winced in pain as he looked at Trina.

"Tell me how bad it is."

Trina tried to avoid his eyes and the question. "How bad is what? Your eyes look much better."

Mark knew in his heart that it must be bad because Trina was trying to avoid his question, so he asked her again. She knew she would not be able to put him off, so she told him.

"You look like you have second degree burns on your back and neck. Most of the hair is gone from the back of your head."

"Thanks for your honesty. If I know what is happening, then I can deal with it. I guess I need to get to a hospital."

The owners had Trina sit in the chair and they once again began the process of cleaning out her eyes. When they had finished, she began to stand up. They held her in the chair. The owner once again began to cut up strips of towels. He then began to cut away her pant leg

"What are you doing that for?" she asked.

The owner looked at her. "Did you know that your leg was injured?"

Trina looked down at her leg. Sticking out of the front of the leg was a piece of metal. It had entered through the back right side of her leg and was sticking out the front about an inch. It had entered right through some of the thickest scar tissue on her legs. It had happened so quick she had not felt it enter. She knew that something was wrong with the leg but chose not to look at it. Now she had to face it. She decided it must have happened when the debris was hitting them.

"Please don't pull it out", she yelled.

"I have no intention of pulling it out. I'm going to wrap something around it so it won't move. That way you'll be able to get to the hospital and have them remove it. I was a medic in the army and so I can fix it so it won't move."

The owner bandaged the leg, being careful not to let the piece of metal move and do more damage. Trina asked if they had a phone she could use. She had lost hers somewhere. He explained to her that he had a phone, but none of the phones were working. The storeowners gave them a cheese sandwich and an ice-cold glass of water. They made them sit, eat, and drink before they allowed them to move on. They felt bad that they had no car and could do nothing else to help them.    Mark and Trina thanked them and then headed back up West Broadway.

Trina had not noticed the pain in her leg until it had been bandaged.  She decided once again to try to put it out of her mind.  She would not let this hinder her.  She noticed the look of pain on Mark's face.  He didn't complain once about the burns on his back.  She knew that he was trying to be brave and not complain for her benefit.  She also knew that if his leg was broken, and she was sure it was, that the pain had to be excruciating.  They had to proceed slowly so they didn't do further damage to it.  It was possible it was just a hairline fracture. They continued to walk north until they reached Canal Street.    Mark thought that if he turned west, he could drag himself through the Holland Tunnel into New Jersey.   He noticed that the police were blocking streets going into the Holland Tunnel.  He stopped an officer and asked what was happening.  The officer told them that they were shutting down all of the bridges and tunnels into Manhattan.  He and Trina asked if he could give them a ride to the hospital.  He told them he would like to but he had orders to stop all traffic from entering the tunnel.  He couldn't leave his station.  Mark and Trina, disappointedly continued heading north.

Mark tried as best he could to block out the pain.  Every step put pressure on the bones.  It was beginning to become almost unbearable.  He knew the shirt was keeping dust from settling onto his back.  It did not matter  the shirt felt soft to the hand.  It felt like someone was taking a scrubby to his back.    He also knew he was going to have to find medical help for himself and for Trina soon.  He could see no way they could continue walking.  As they neared New York University, Trina suggested they stop to see if they could use the phones.  They noticed the campus was deserted.  They tried the doors only to find them locked.  They had shut the campus down.  Trina sat down on the steps and began to cry.  She could not believe no one would stop for them, or help them.  How were they ever going to get home?

Why was everything going wrong this day? She sat for a few minutes, allowing herself to have a small pity party. She bowed her head and said a quiet prayer. After a couple of minutes, she stood up and decided that she had pitied her situation enough, and it was time to move on. After all, she had decided that she was, and always would be a survivor.

Trina and Mark continued up West Broadway until they reached West Fourth Street. They turned west and dragged themselves along until they reached Avenue of the Americas. They periodically tried to flag someone down for help, but no one stopped for them. They could see the panic and terror in the eyes of those who passed them by. There was no trust left. That had all blown away when the planes hit the towers. It was possible that these people were just trying to find their own loved ones. They traveled north until they reached St. Vincent's Hospital.

The nurse sitting at the admitting desk looked up and saw two dusty figures coming in the door. She knew immediately that she was seeing people who had been down in the area of the Twin Towers. The young girl looked familiar, but it was hard to tell with so much dust. As they approached, the nurse quickly stood up. She knew this girl. This was Doctor Lacy's daughter, Trina. She rushed around the desk to help the two young people. She had them both sit in wheelchairs. She quickly assessed their injuries, and she and another nurse took them ahead of others waiting patiently in the waiting room. Trina was sure someone would say something. People looked from the television to the two teens and back at the television. There was a sense of shock and pity in their eyes. No one said a word. It was almost an unspoken rule that if they had survived the collapse of the World Trade Center, then they had been through enough and had earned the right to go first.

The nurse took them to two empty rooms in the back and paged Trina's father to the emergency room. When he called to find out what the emergency was, the nurse informed him that

91

his daughter had just walked in with a friend and both of them were injured. He practically ran to the emergency room.

"Daddy", Trina cried. She had not called him daddy since she was little. She needed to be his little girl and let him take care of her. He held her for a long while, rocking her in his arms feeling the trembling of her body. When she had cried herself out and calmed down, she told him what had happened.

"I met Mark on the way down the stairs, and when we were escaping the building it began to collapse. He tried to protect me by covering me with his body. Please daddy, check on Mark, because he was badly burned."

"I will baby, just as soon as the doctors come in here and take care of you. You know I can't treat you, because you're my daughter. Were you able to meet up with your aunt?"

Trina looked at him and began to cry. He assumed the worst had happened.

"A computer fell off of her desk, and hit her in the head. We headed down the stairs. She was having a lot of trouble walking, so two men picked her up and carried her down the stairs. I don't know what happened to her. I'm not sure if she got out of the building. She was ahead of me so she should have gotten out. I am so sorry I can't tell you what happened to her."

He hugged her tight telling her that she had nothing for which to apologize. He was sure her aunt had made it out, and that she was safe in another hospital. One of the emergency room doctors entered her room and began to examine her. He told her father that he would let him know what he had found when he had finished examining her. Her father took one last look at her, gave her another hug, then he let the other doctor take care of her. He stepped next door to check on Mark.

As Doctor Lacy walked into Marks room, he saw a young man who was obviously in a lot of pain. Doctor Stuart was checking out his burns.

"Hello. You must be Mark. I am Doctor Lacy, Trina's father. Trina told me that you helped her out of the building. I want to shake your hand and thank you for saving my daughter's life. She also told me that you've suffered burns on your back protecting her. I can never thank you enough for bringing her back to us once again."

Mark leaned forward letting the doctors examine his burned back. "When we were trying to get to the hospital we stopped in at a small store to get some water. The storeowner and his wife treated our eyes and bandaged our wounds. The man gave me a clean shirt because my shirt burned right off my back. I wish I knew their names so that I could thank them."

Dr. Lacy listened and prayed silently that God would bless the couple that had come to the aid of these young people. He assured Mark that he would be okay. He looked at the leg as the other doctor ordered an x-ray while waiting to transfer him to the burn unit. He was sure that the leg was broken. What was unclear was how Mark had managed to walk as far as he had on that leg. What was his motivation? He had seen grown men sit down and give up. Why had they not just sat down and waited until help could come to them? They brought the portable x-ray machine in and took an x-ray confirming it was broken. They temporarily immobilized it so that they would be able to deal with his burns first. That was their biggest concern. They gave Mark a shot of morphine to help with the pain. As he began to drift off, they began the painful process of cleaning the burns. Buried deep into the burned tissue were pieces of glass, metal and other unidentifiable things. They carefully, and as quickly as possible, cleaned the wounds. They put a soothing salve and clean dressing on the burns. When they had finished with the burns, they started on his leg. They reviewed the x-rays and then set his leg. A cast finished the job. They wheeled him to a room in the burn unit. Every few hours someone came in, changed his dressing, and gave him more morphine.

Trina's father tried to reach his wife on her cell phone. It seemed that all of the lines were down. He tried her office again and got no answer. His pager went off. He recognized the number of his daughter's school. He answered only to hear the strained voice of his wife. She was near hysterics. She told him she had been trying to reach Trina on her cell phone all morning but had been unable to get through.     Someone at work had come in and told her that a plane had hit Tower One, of the World Trade Center. It was then she had started calling Trina's phone and her sister's office. She had been in another office when the towers had started to come down. She told him she thought that maybe Trina would try to get to the school, or her office, so she had left someone at the office and gone to the school.     She took a deep breath and her husband used the opportunity to interrupt her.

"Trina is safe.     She and Mark came walking into the emergency room a little while ago. She is dirty, bruised up and has a leg injury, but nothing life threatening. Her friend Mark has a broken leg and second degree burns down the back of his head to his waist.     She said he protected her when the ash and debris from the collapsing building caught up to them. They'd been running, tripped over something and fell. She had landed next to a car that had shielded most of her body. Mark had protected her from the flames that came shooting through the dust cloud.     She was able to crawl out and help remove the debris that had fallen on top of him. He saved our little girl. He seems like such a nice young man. I got the name and phone number of his aunt and uncle in New Jersey. I called them but they are unable to get here."

"The authorities have shut down Manhattan. They're going to try to find some way to get here. Trina said your sister was hurt when the first plane hit the towers. Some men carried her down and hopefully out of the building, but she doesn't know where your sister is. Maybe you could call the different hospitals and see if she's at one of them. Will you let the school know that the kids are safe? I know that they've heard the news and they must be very concerned knowing that their fellow students had been in the building."

"Are they all safe?  When did you hear from Lucas?"

"Lucas? Oh no, I forgot about Lucas. He hasn't been brought into the hospital and Trina told me she'd heard from him while she was in Tower One. He was on his way down from Tower Two. Please call his parents and see if they've heard anything. Since they've started closing down lower Manhattan, they won't be able to get into the city. The ferry is no longer bringing people from the island. I'll see you when you get here. Have them page me."

He hung up and went back to the room where they held his daughter. The doctors were getting her ready for surgery to remove the piece of shrapnel from her leg. He signed the necessary papers and walked with her to the operating room. He told her that they had already taken care of Mark. He said a prayer with her, and kissed her before they took her into surgery.

# 13 The Wait

Mr. and Mrs. James sat on the couch watching the news footage of the day's events. Four planes had crashed, and the terrorists took thousands of lives. They sat numbly waiting for the phone to ring. They prayed that it would be their son, and not someone calling to give them bad news. The newscaster had said the ferry was not taking anyone to Manhattan, and most of Manhattan was shut down. They did not know how they would get to their son if he needed them. They were so startled when the phone began to ring they sat staring at it, praying Lucas was on the other end.

"Hello?" answered Mr. James.

"Mr. James? This is Mrs. Lacy, Trina's mother. My husband just called me from the hospital. Trina and Mark came in about a half hour ago. They asked me to call you to see if you've heard from Lucas. Trina said she had talked to him as he was on his way down the stairs in the South Tower. She hasn't heard from him since that time and hoped that you had."

Mr. James began to silently cry. His back was to his wife so she could not see the tears once again flowing slowly down his cheeks. She knew he was crying because his shoulders had begun to tremble. He feared the worst. He coughed, as if trying to clear his throat and answered Mrs. Lacy.

"No Mrs. Lacy, we haven't heard from Lucas. We're very concerned about his whereabouts. We've tried his phone, but can't get through. We've heard that they've closed down most of Manhattan, and the ferry is no longer running. Please, if you hear anything, let us know. We're stuck here on Staten Island and can't get into the city. What are Mark and Trina's conditions? Are they okay?"

"Mark has burns on his back and neck and a broken leg. Trina suffered an injury to her leg, but she'll be just fine. I'll let you know if I hear anything." She gave them her cell number and the number of the hospital in case they heard from Lucas so that they could keep in touch. She told them that she would say a prayer for his safety. She hung up, updated the principal of Eagle Prep, and then headed for St. Vincent's Hospital.

Lucas and Ken continued walking up Church Street. They stopped often and asked if anyone had a telephone they could use. The phone service was spotty everywhere, it seemed. The day's events seemed to have brought out the kindness in people. Business owners offered bottles of water, while others offered them a meal. Lucas wanted to get Ken to his wife and sons but he knew it was important to keep his strength up. So far, he had only had two cups of coffee. One was at the country club with his father, and the other one was at the Coffee Station with Trina and Mark. He wondered where they were and if they were okay. He had seen his distorted reflection in the dust covered windows and knew that he looked terrible. He didn't understand why so many people were staring and pointing at him. He knew he still had the dusty ash on him like so many others. As they passed a mother and her young child, he learned what the problem was.

"Look mommy, his back is cut and there is something sticking out."

The mother hushed the child and pulled her away. Lucas stopped Ken.

"What exactly, is wrong with my back? Why is everyone looking at me and pointing? What haven't you told me?"

"Well, remember when you shielded me with your body?"

"Yes, I remember. My shirt was shredded by all of the debris."

"Yes, it was shredded. I figured if you couldn't feel it, I wouldn't mention it until we got to a hospital."

Lucas looked at Ken with concern. "What exactly is wrong with my back?"

"You have several pieces of metal embedded in your back. Some of them entered one place and came out in another. I know that you thought your back was cut up pretty bad. I didn't want to say anything because a doctor needs to remove them. I figured if I could convince you to get me to the hospital because of my wife, that they would fix your back, and you wouldn't worry about it until then. If I've caused you to worry, I am sorry. That was not my intention."

"You haven't caused me to worry. I appreciate your honesty. Knowing the way I am, I probably would have tried to remove it. I guess it's a good thing that the windows have been dirty. I couldn't see it. How bad do you think it is? You need to tell me because if you don't, then I'll think about it non-stop all the way to the hospital."

"One of the pieces has entered near your spine. That is why I didn't want you to know. I don't know why you're not feeling any of it."

"I didn't say I wasn't feeling anything. I didn't figure it would help your heart if you had to worry about the pain I was feeling. I thought my back was scraped up pretty good and that was why it was burning. You know, like when you fall on asphalt and scrape your knees. I also assumed, I had pulled some muscles to go along with the ribs. You could have told me I looked like some reject from another planet. After all, I was trying to impress all of the pretty girls."

They laughed together and headed north. When they reached Canal Street, their luck changed. A cab driver took one look at them and pulled over. He got out and helped Ken into the car. Lucas got in the car, careful not to sit back. He asked the driver to take them to St. Vincent's hospital. As the driver drove to the hospital, Lucas began to chuckle. He had noticed how careful the cab driver was with his driving, something unusual for a New York City cab driver. He tried not to make any sharp turns or hit any major bumps. It was almost as if he was carrying the most precious cargo in the world. Ken asked him what was so funny. Lucas told him this was the safest taxi ride he had ever taken. Ken joined him in the laughter. They pulled up to the emergency room. As they stepped out of the car, Lucas reached for his wallet. The driver stopped him.

"I could not take any money from you. I'm just paying back a debt. My sister was in the South Tower this morning. She said some young man saved her. She called me and asked me if I would help by going down and bringing people out of the area. They've closed the lower part of Manhattan down, so I've been going as far as they will let me, picking people up to take them wherever they need to go. I just hope that sometime today I will pick up her young man so that I can thank him. I love my niece Sasha, but I don't want to have to raise her because she lost her mother. She's already lost her daddy."

Lucas looked at the driver and held out his hand to him. "Tell Cassie that Lucas said you have repaid the debt."

"You are the young man", he cried. He grabbed his hand and shook it vigorously.

Ken smiled at Lucas and told him that they needed to go in and get themselves looked at. The cab driver thanked him again, then he returned to his cab and left to help more people. Lucas followed Ken inside. Ken walked up to the counter. The nurse looked up and saw the dust covered bodies before her. She recognized the haunted look in their eyes. She asked them to follow her to an area set up for victims from the World Trade Center. They had only had a few cases. This realization was depressing. With such mass destruction, everyone was sure there would be more survivors.

She ushered the two of them down the hallway and toward a room. As they passed the waiting room Lucas suddenly heard his name called. He stopped and looked behind him. Running toward him was Trina's mother. She grabbed him and hugged him. He cried out in pain. She released him and stepped back.

"I must call your parents and let them know you're here and safe. They've been so worried about all of you. I'll check in with you in just a little while."

Lucas thanked her and left with the nurse.

The phone rang and Mr. and Mrs. James cautiously answered it. Mrs. Lacy was speaking so quickly and excitedly that they had to ask her to repeat what she had said. They listened to her, hung up the phone and hugged each other. They were excited and relieved to hear that Lucas was okay. Mrs. Lacy had told them that he was injured, but he had walked in on his own, and she didn't think it was very serious. She told them that she would call them as soon as she had heard anything from the doctors. Once again, all they could do was play the waiting game.

Mr. James went to the kitchen and poured coffee for the two of them. He brought it into the living room and sat next to his wife. He had a serious look on his face.

"Are you happy with your life?" he asked.

"I am happy. At times, I am also sad. What I mean is that I miss my life of dance. I don't want to travel the world the way I once had. I want to stay home. However, I would love to teach a dance class. I have wanted this more than anything, for several years."

"Why didn't you tell me this?"

"I have mentioned this to you several times, but you brushed it aside. Your comment was always, 'what would our friends think about you working'. I personally never cared what they thought, but you did."

Mr. James hung his head. "I am so sorry. I've done this to you, and to Lucas. I've not really let you live. I made you live my life. I pretty much took yours away from you. Now, I've been given a second chance to make things right, and that is just what I plan on doing."

He stood up and ran his hand through his hair. "I don't know how much longer I can stand to wait here in this house. I know the control freak in me wants to be in control over something that I have absolutely no control over. My son and his friends are in the hospital, and we have no way of reaching them." His wife stood up and hugged him.

"We'll get through this, I promise you."

Mark's aunt and uncle had tried every number they could think of. They were looking for answers. How long before they could enter Manhattan to go to the hospital and see Mark? They'd heard nothing else from Trina's parents so they sat silently on their porch. The events of the day made them remember the night of the fire. They had received a call that night from the police telling them what had happened. They told the officers that they would most definitely take their nephew in to live with them. Now here they were with their nephew in the burn unit at St. Vincent's Hospital. It seemed ironic that a fire was the cause of his parents' death, and he lay in a hospital burned. They did not know what they would do, if they lost Mark. They felt the same helplessness that they had felt the night of the fire. It had been a constant fear from that day on that they would lose Mark, as they had his parents. That nightmare had almost come true today at the hands of terrorists who could care less about life. They could not wait to get their hands on him, and to let him know how much they loved him.

Mrs. Lacy sat alone in the waiting room. Her husband would be off duty in a few short minutes and would join her. She took the time to reflect on the day's events. She bowed her head and prayed for all of the families who didn't have the closure that she and her husband had. She had only experienced the panic of not knowing where her child was for a few hours. There were people who would have to wait until rescuers could reach their loved ones, if that was at all possible.

She thanked God, for protecting the three young people who had such promising lives before them. Then she prayed for her sister. She did not know what had happened to her. She had called all of the hospitals in Manhattan. She knew that they should have taken her to one of the closest hospitals. She prayed that maybe she had amnesia and didn't know who she was. She figured she could wait until her husband joined her, and then she would start calling the hospitals in Brooklyn and New Jersey.

# 14  A Time of Healing

Dr. Lacy came into the room and told his wife that Trina was out of surgery. The piece of metal had not done any major damage. They had been able to remove it and stitch it up. He said the reason she hadn't felt it enter her leg was that it had pierced an area full of scar tissue from her burns. She was so focused on Mark, she hadn't even noticed it. He filled her in on Mark's condition. He reminded his wife that they had been through the burn process with Trina.

"I told Mark that we would be here for him the same way we had been here for Trina. He asked me if his burns were as bad as hers were. I assured him they were not as severe. Had he had his blazer on, his head would have been the only part of him that would have been burned. The blazer would have taken the majority of the heat."

Dr. Lacy chuckled. "As he was beginning to drift off, from the morphine, he said something like, 'I guess I won't be going back for my jacket any time soon'. I asked him where it was. He said he had left it on the handrail in the North Tower. I assured him that there was no need to go back because it was no longer there. I also looked in on Lucas. It seems like he is going to be stuck here for a few days as well. If you will give me his parent's number, I will call them and give them an update. The old man he came in with, was just slightly scraped and bruised. I admitted him because he'd been having chest pains after walking down all of those stairs. He is now comfortably sharing a room with his wife on the cardiac floor. She's one of my patients, and now so is he."

Unexpectedly his beeper went off. Who would be calling him now? They knew he had just gone off duty. They also knew that he had just checked in on his daughter and their friends, and they were fine. He looked at his beeper with a concerned and puzzled look.

"I have to call this number and then I'll be right back."

He stepped over to the phone and dialed the number. He had recognized it but could not understand why the morgue would be calling him. Had one of his patients died? If this was the case then they should have been able to reach him. He identified himself and then listened intently to the message. He hung up the phone and looked across the room at his wife. He went to her and explained he had to check on something and that he would return in about fifteen minutes or so. He walked quickly out of the room. She smiled at him lovingly. She recognized the pained look in his eyes. She had seen it before when he had lost one of his patients. She hoped it was not the woman or the older man that he had just discussed.

She decided to start calling the hospitals in Brooklyn and across the river in New Jersey, to see if they had her sister. It was during her third call that she noticed her husband standing in the doorway. It was obvious that he had been crying. He came to her and wrapped his arms around her. She knew then that whatever it was, it had to be bad. He sat her down on the couch and faced her.

"It's your sister. She's here."

"Thank goodness you found her. How bad is she hurt? Can I see her or do I need to wait?" Nervously she rattled on. "Did they say where she has been all this time?"

She waited for him to answer. In his silence, she realized the reason for the tears. She looked at him in horror. She had suddenly become one of those, for whom she had been praying. She was one of those who had lost someone due to a cruel act of terrorism. She began to wail. Her husband grabbed her and held her tight. He rocked her back and forth and let her cry until she could cry no more. At first, they were tears of pain. The pain of losing someone she was so close to. Her sister had been her best friend, her confidant. They had done everything together. If her sister tried a new craft, then it was not long before she was trying it. If her sister visited an interesting place then it was not long before she would visit it. Who would fill that void? Her parents

103

were dead. She had no other brothers or sisters. She was alone. Sure, she had her husband and her daughter, but she would never again have her sister.

The tears soon turned into tears of anger. She directed her anger at the senseless, uncaring animals that had taken the lives of so many innocent people, including her sister. How could they be so cruel? How could they not think about the families they had destroyed? It tore her up when she thought about all that was lost. Her sister had not married, figuring she still had time, and then her life was over. This was a blessing as she left behind no children. How many children were going to bed this night, not knowing if they had lost one or both of their parents? She blew her nose and then looked at her husband.

"What happened? Trina said that two men carried her down from the North Tower. She didn't pass her aunt in the stairway so how did she end up dead?"

"They found her in the ambulance. They had just loaded her into the ambulance when the South Tower came down. They had found the driver next to his door, she and the paramedic were inside. The ambulance was crushed by debris from the South Tower. We can wait until later to tell Trina. Let her have one night of peace. I know her well enough that she will blame herself for her aunt's death. You and I know that there was nothing she could have done to have helped her."

Dr. Lacy asked his wife if she would be okay while he called Lucas' parents. She told him she would. He left the room. A few minutes later an off duty nurse came in with a cup of coffee. The nurse informed her, that her husband had asked her to sit with his wife while he was gone. She thanked the nurse for her kindness.

Dr. Lacy dialed the number for the James' home. Mr. James answered on the first ring. He listened as Dr. Lacy told him about his son's injuries. He had talked with Lucas before he had gone into surgery and he had quite a story to tell his parents.

"Your son ended up with three broken ribs and two cracked ribs. They took him into surgery to remove the debris. They were concerned because he had a large piece of metal right next to his spine. However, they were able to remove it with no damage to his spinal cord. They're going to keep him for a couple of days to make sure there's no infection. I know that you and your wife are unable to get in here because they've closed down the city. My wife and I will be staying here all night. We'll look in on him from time to time. I think it will do her good. She lost her sister today when the South Tower collapsed, so she needs to feel useful and keep busy. If there are any changes we'll call you." He answered a few more questions from Mr. James and hung up. He walked back into the waiting room and thanked the nurse for waiting with his wife.

"I reached Lucas' father and explained his injuries. I told him we would be spending the night here and that we would look in on him. Mark's in isolation because of his burns. I've asked them to put recliners in Trina and Lucas' rooms. Which room would you like to sleep in? I don't want either of them to wake up and have no one there. Mark will be kept out with the morphine most of the night so there's no worry there."

Mrs. Lacy looked knowingly at her husband. He knew her so well. This would not take away the pain of her loss but it would help her heal knowing she was helping someone else. "I know how I would feel if I couldn't get up here to be with Trina. I know she would want her mother to be near her so I'll sleep in Lucas' room if you don't mind. He needs to have a mother figure with him. Besides, I think his mother would want that."

Time seemed to pass slowly. Trina woke up in the middle of the night. Her father was sleeping in a chair next to her bed. She remembered seeing him like this many nights after she had left the burn unit. Something woke him up.

"Was I snoring?" he asked.

"No daddy, I was thirsty." He handed her a drink of water.

"Not sleepy pumpkin?"

She could tell his stress level by his calling her pumpkin.

"Not really. I keep thinking about all of those people that were in the Towers when they came down. Do you think they knew what was happening? Did it hurt?"

He wanted to protect her from all of the terrible things in the world. He knew that there was no way he could protect her from this. She had lived through this, so he answered her honestly.

"I think when the rumbling started, those close to the bottom of the building or right outside had time to think about what was happening. Did it hurt? I doubt it. They are saying on the news that the buildings took about ten seconds to collapse. That is approximately eleven floors every second. They didn't have time to feel anything. I know that doesn't really make you feel any better. I don't think any of us will feel better for quite some time."

"Why, dad? Why did it happen? What caused the planes to fly into the buildings?"

"It was terrorists, Trina. They cared only about killing as many people as they could. They flew planes into both Towers, the Pentagon, and they had another plane. The passengers on that plane managed to overpower them and crash it into the ground so the terrorists could not kill anyone else but those on the plane. They sacrificed their lives for others. We'll never forget this day. We must never forget it, for those who were brave and survived, like you, Mark, and Lucas. By the way, Lucas has turned into quite an awesome young man. It seems that he helped save a young single mother, and then he saved an old man, whose wife is one of my patients. He did all of this while suffering injuries twice. I think you two need to sit down sometime soon and talk. Life is too short to hold grudges. You need to hold on to all of those you love or have loved."

Trina saw the faraway look in her father's eyes, and she knew that something was wrong. He had such a sad look on his face. It was almost as if he had lost someone.

"Dad, is it Mark? Did something happen to Mark?"

"No honey, he is doing just fine."

"Who is it dad, and don't lie to me. Your face tells it all."

Dr. Lacy looked down at the floor, then up at his daughter. "They found your aunt today. She made it out of the building. When the South Tower collapsed it fell on the ambulance she was in and she was killed instantly."

Trina looked at her father. Tears slid down her cheeks. She had felt it for quite some time. Somehow, she knew, and it was okay. She was glad that she had been with her aunt. At least she had been with her to help her during this trying day.

"It's okay dad. I felt it in my heart all day. When I didn't see her and couldn't find her, I knew. How is mom doing?"

"She's holding up okay. Right now, she's asleep in Lucas' room. Mark is out for a while. You remember how it was with you."

"What about their parents? Are they here yet?

"Manhattan has essentially been shut down. They have closed all of the tunnels and all of the bridges. Security is very tight right now. They grounded planes all over the United States until further notice. This is not just affecting people here in New York or Washington D.C., it is affecting people all over the world. There is hope that their parents will be allowed in the city within the next few hours."

He encouraged his daughter to go back to sleep. Once he was sure she was sound asleep, he left her room to check on Mark and Lucas. Both of them seemed to be doing fine. He checked with the nurses to see if there was any change so he could update their families. He checked his wife and found that she was sleeping. He knew that the next few days would be tough for her. He also knew that they would rely on their faith once again to bring them through these tough times. He checked his watch. It was five-thirty in the morning. He went into the waiting room and sat before the television to see if there was anything new about the events of the day before. He could see police and firefighters checking the burning rubble for survivors. He looked at the pictures and wondered how anyone could survive that mess. He learned that several firefighters had been found alive in a stairway. According to the news, they had stopped to help a woman who could walk no further. They refused to leave her. Exhausted she stopped for a brief rest. The Tower crumbled around them. They had survived. He hoped for more miracles from the disaster area. He closed his eyes for just a minute. The next thing he knew his wife was by his side with a cup of coffee. He had been asleep for two hours. He checked on his daughter and her friends, then called their families and gave them an update.

Mrs. James had been up for quite some time. She felt terrible for Mrs. Lacy's loss. She watched the news. Hundreds of people wandered the street putting up flyers. They were looking for their loved ones, the ones who had never come home. At least Mrs. Lacy knew what had happened to her sister. She knew that waiting for word was the hardest thing you could do. She had lived that nightmare yesterday.

She decided to fix some breakfast for her husband before they left for the hospital. They had opened a couple of bridges, so they could get in to see Lucas. Identification was necessary to enter the city.

Mark groggily looked around the room. He saw a couple of funny looking people in a mask and gown. He thought they were funny looking because they were his aunt and uncle. He was so glad to see them. It had seemed like an eternity since he had last seen them. There was a time that he was unsure he would ever see them again. His aunt came near his bed.

"They told us not to touch you yet. I can't wait to hug you", she said.

"Once I am out of here, I'll gladly let you hug me all you want. There was a time yesterday when I was afraid I would never see you again. I saw so much. It didn't seem to matter how much I tried to do, there was so much that was out of my control. Trina and I talked about that a lot. She told me that I was experiencing survivor's guilt, because I had survived and my parents had not. I don't know why Trina and I survived and others around us didn't. I don't have to know. I just have to thank God that he gave me another day to live. Speaking of living, you know what sounds good right about now?"

His aunt looked at him and replied, "A bagel with strawberry cream cheese?"

Mark began to laugh. "Ugh! No! I don't want that ever again. I ate it only because my mom had loved it. Personally, I hated it. I would love to have an ice cold glass of water."

His aunt stepped out of the room to get a nurse to bring him some water. While she was gone, his uncle took the opportunity to tell Mark how glad he was that he had made it out. He told him that he may be their nephew but they thought of him as the son they never had. This made tears come to Mark's eyes. His uncle was a man of few words. He usually showed very little emotion. His face showed Mark all the emotions he had missed over the previous months. He knew that his life had changed. He was a survivor. He could say that now, and know that it was okay.

Lucas was sitting up in bed when his parents walked in. Sitting in a chair next to him in a hospital gown was an older man. He started to stand up and they told him to remain seated.

"You must be the parents of this wonderful young man", Mr. Graham said. If it hadn't been for your son, I wouldn't be here today. My wife is in this hospital. My sons had been visiting with her while I went to the office to get some papers. The planes hit the building and I walked out. Your son took a beating trying to save my sorry hide", said Mr. Graham, "and I am very grateful to him." He began to choke up.

"It is sad to say that I've heard several people tell me how special my son is, and I didn't recognize it in him until today. I believe I need to have my eyes checked. I don't know how I could have been so blind all this time. I never saw my son's potential. I always expected a certain thing from him. Now I see him as a man. The things he had done yesterday are the things that made him a man. Thank you for being there with my son so that he didn't have to go through this terrible thing by himself. I don't know if I can every thank you enough."

Lucas interrupted them. "I love all of the sentiment, but, how about some food, maybe a little steak and eggs." Everyone began to laugh.

Mr. Graham got up from his chair. "I best get back upstairs to my wife before they come looking for me. I went AWOL. I figured I best check on this young man while the nurses were away and the wife was asleep."

As he walked out of the door, a young woman came in.

"Cassie, you came to see me. How's Sasha? Did your brother tell you he picked me up and brought me to the hospital? How cool was that, and what a coincidence!"

Cassie laughed; she turned and introduced herself to Lucas' parents. She explained how Lucas had helped her get home to her daughter. She told Lucas that all of the men from her husband's station had survived. They'd gotten there after the building collapsed and had been working tirelessly trying to find survivors. They had sent several of their wives to her house to make sure she was okay. Even though her husband was gone, they would always consider her and her daughter family. She thanked his parents for raising such a wonderful and caring young man and then she left them alone.

Lucas' face turned red with embarrassment as he grinned at his parents. He didn't really know what to say.

# 15 Changes

Tragedy changes lives. Mark, Trina, and Lucas had all experienced tragedy and change first hand. Trina limped, to Mark's room. "I'll visit you as often as I'm allowed. I'll also make sure someone from Angel Hope will be with you two or three times a week. I expected you to never give up. You need to remember that you're a survivor and not a victim."

Mark started to laugh at her. "Seems to me I remember some parts of this conversation in the elevator, and when you were helping me up off of the ground. I think I have it down now."

Trina smiled at him. "If I didn't have this stupid mask on, I'd kiss you. I was so full of self-doubt about everything before all of this happened. Afraid of living, I eliminated the fun in my life and focused on other things. For all of my talk of not being a victim, I had turned myself into one. Thank you for being a good friend and helping me realize that it's okay to live again."

Mark looked at her thoughtfully. "I think we all changed that day. I had to learn that I couldn't control everything. Some things are way out of our hands. I couldn't control the planes crashing into the buildings and killing all of those people. I couldn't control the injuries I sustained. I learned that I couldn't have controlled the outcome of the fire that took my parents. However, I can control the way that I react to situations. I could choose to hate the men who did this. I've learned that hatred just eats at our insides. It doesn't matter if that hatred is directed at others or yourself. It does nothing to them. I choose to be in control of my attitude. I choose not to hate, because that's what drove them to fly the planes into the Towers. I'm a survivor. One thing I do have control over, is the choice to ask my new best friend for that kiss when I get out of here, and for a possible date."

Trina laughed, "Deal." She left his room, and headed down the hall to see Lucas.

"Trina, what are you doing here? I was just packing my things and getting ready to head home, as soon as they release me."

Trina took a deep breath. "I came to tell you that they're letting me go home. My father talked with me last night, and suggested I sit down and talk with you. I guess after the accident I didn't really give you much of a chance to say anything to me. I didn't want to hear your side of the story. You tried so hard to apologize to me. I made sure that I constantly gave you the cold shoulder. If you had died in the collapse of that building, then I would have felt terribly guilty. I would have let a good friend die without him knowing that I cared for him. I want to be your friend. At this time, that is all I can offer you. I'm sorry for not giving you a chance sooner. We lost so much valuable time because of my attitude. Would you please forgive me?"

"I think I am the one who needs to ask your forgiveness", said Mr. James, as he entered the room. "I'm sorry to interrupt but I need to apologize to you, and to Lucas. I've wanted the best for my son for a long time. I thought I knew what was best for him, even if he didn't agree with me. I am so sorry for what I said outside of your room in the hospital. You thought you'd heard Lucas. What you actually heard was our argument and Lucas throwing my words back at me. He never felt you were ugly due to your burns. He argued that point quite well. I refused to listen. He was right about one thing though. I was always afraid of what other people would think. I need to ask the both of you to forgive me."

Trina walked over to him and hugged him. "I forgive you Mr. James."

"I promise you both that you will see many changes in me. Lucas, your mother has been talking to me and it is my understanding that you want to become a P.E. teacher. What do you say that when we get home we start researching the best colleges to help you achieve that goal?"

Lucas looked at his father completely stunned by what he had heard. "All right, who are you, and what did you do with my father? Are you sure you're my real father?"

Mr. James laughed, "Yes, I'm sure. By the way, you're going to have to give up your apartment and move back into the house with your mother and me. We're turning your apartment into a dance studio for your mother. She'd like to start giving ballet lessons. That means that you and I are going to have to pick up some of the slack around the house and help her out."

"Like I said, who are you and what did you do with my father? Don't get me wrong. I like all of the changes. It just seems weird hearing all of this come from you."

"I know son, it's been too long since I acted like the loving father and husband, that I once was. It's time that I make the changes before it's too late. Yesterday's events showed me how precious time is and how things can be gone in just a blink of the eye. I had a lot of time to really sit and think last night while you were in the hospital. I think I knew these things deep down inside of me. I just refused to acknowledge them before last night." Lucas hugged his father. He had a new admiration for him.

Over the next few days, there were several changes to Manhattan. The skyline was forever changed. The clean up of the Twin Towers and surrounding buildings was just beginning. They found no one else alive. Families continued to hang up fliers asking for help in finding their missing loved ones. Memorials sprang up all over the area. Children and other people from around the world sent cards, letters, shirts and banners to the area they now called 'Ground Zero'. Crowds visited daily. The terrorists had set out to change the world and lives of Americans. They had succeeded, but not in the way they intended. They had changed Americans from a complacent people to a stronger people, who decided they would not be victims, but survivors.

Trina and Lucas returned to school. Twice a week they collected homework for Mark. They continued to be leaders at school, and in the community. They completed the community service project they had been working on the day the Towers collapsed. Mr. Graham helped accomplish this. He contacted many of the businesses that had survived the collapse of the Twin Towers. He told the heroic story of three young people and the Angel Hope project for which they had almost lost their lives. With his help, they surpassed their original goal of three hundred thousand dollars. They presented a check to the Angel Hope Charity for five hundred and fifty thousand dollars. The students at Eagle Prep voted early to make Trina the Valedictorian of their senior class. She told Mark and Lucas that she would make sure that the students knew they needed to remember the past events and make changes to their lives, while looking to the future and making changes in the lives of others. They would remember all of the people who had helped them, those hidden angels, and pay it forward. They would enter the world as survivors, teaching this lesson to others.

# 16 Choices

Trina had stayed true to her mission to educate students everywhere. She often found herself in an auditorium giving a talk about what it means to be a survivor. At first, the memories were painful. The pain and death she saw that day would be with her forever. Talking about the event was actually healing for her. She had kept the details of her accident bottled up for so long thinking that if she just tried to put it behind her she could move on with her life. Life she found out does not work that way. Her ordeal in the Twin Towers was not like her accident. The accident had been tough to deal with. She had to come to terms with her own frailty after the accident. Now she had to face the memories of those who lost their lives in the towers. She went through survivor's guilt like everyone else. She had nightmares where she saw the panicked faces of those in the towers with her, faces of those who lost their lives. She dreamed of those who ran beside her from the building, suddenly swept away by the debris. Night after night she woke up shaking, wondering if she could have done something to save just one of them. The faces and event haunted her. She decided she must face the issues no matter how hard they were, and then she had to work her way through them, one step at a time. It seemed strange that almost two years had gone by since the events that had changed the face of America and its people.

Trina sat in the offices of Angel Hope where she volunteered on weekends. She had checked her assignments for visiting the burn unit and thought about how her life had changed, and the way her whole career decision had come about because of 9/11. Her father had always encouraged her to go into the medical field. He was actually hoping she would become a doctor like himself. She had already completed all of her hours to become an LPN, or Licensed Practical Nurse. She would be heading back to school in a little over a week. Somehow, she would have to try balancing her nursing classes with her work in the burn unit at the hospital. She knew it would be tough to get everything done to earn her degree to become a registered nurse. Then, she would have at least another year to earn her Master of Science in critical care so she could be a specialized nurse in the burn unit.

Her friends at school could not understand her drive. After spending so much time in a burn unit after her accident, they thought sure she would want to stay away from one. Here she was moving toward it. She had this aching desire to continue on this course of action. She wanted to make sure she was there to help others. Since she had been in their shoes, she felt she would be better qualified to help. She felt blessed that her mother and father supported her in her decision. Without their support, she did not know if she could make it. It had been a tough ride after the death of her aunt in the collapse. She realized it could have been either one of them injured in the towers and carried down. She and her family were grateful they had been able to recover her aunt's body. So many people were still waiting for any sign of their loved one so they could have some closure. Even now as cleanup continued at ground zero pieces of bone, were occasionally discovered. When this happened a horn sounded and the site went silent. They treated the recovered bone fragment with the same respect with which a complete body was treated.

Trina left the Angel Hope offices and walked the three blocks to the hospital going straight for the burn unit. Her most recent patient was a twelve-year-old named Emily. She was inside of her house during a fire. Her seventeen-year-old neighbor heard her screams and dove through her window to rescue her. He had no idea that the added oxygen would cause the room to flash over. He had literally tossed her through the window before diving back through. A neighbor was spraying both of them down with a water hose as the fire department pulled up. As the rescuers were telling him how stupid it was for him to go into such a dangerous situation without the proper knowledge of a firefighter, they were also commending him for saving the girl's life. The young girl had been in the extremely hot, and smoky room longer than he had, and had suffered more severe burns. He did not seem concerned with the scars he would have. When the newspaper had asked him why he had gone in, and if he had been afraid, his answer was simple.

"I was terrified and who wouldn't be? I didn't want to burn. However, I most definitely didn't want to live the rest of my life seeing Emily's face and hearing her scream as she burned to death, because just a few feet separated us. I knew I might be able to do something. Even though I was afraid, her screams moved me to action. My cuts from going through the window were almost worse than my burns. I'm just glad we both got out alive."

Trina had smiled at his selflessness when she had seen the interview. She had been up to visit him a couple of days after he had arrived. Michael was a nice looking young man. He had the prettiest eyes she had ever seen. Their deep russet color contrasted beautifully with his black hair. They had a playfulness to them that made Trina think that he probably got anything he wanted, most of the time.

As Trina walked into Emily's room, she found Michael sitting in a wheelchair next to Emily's bed. He was a constant visitor. He treated her as if she was his little sister, her protector.

"Oh I can see right now that this is not good", she teased.

"Michael came to see me and make sure I'm doing okay." Trina watched Emily flutter her long lashes in Michael's direction. Oh, this girl had a bad crush on Michael, and either Michael was oblivious to it, or he was good at ignoring it.

"Well, since Michael is here I can talk with both of you at the same time. Michael I hear you're going to be released?"

Trina heard a whimper from Emily. She had assumed Michael had already told Emily.

"Listen, I have to go back to my room so maybe you can stop in and get your answer there." He quickly whirled around in his wheelchair and left Emily's room.

"Well that was strange", Trina muttered, noting the way Michael avoided the subject in front of Emily. She turned back to Emily and saw the tears slide down her cheeks.

"Trina, why didn't he tell me? Why does he get to go home and I don't?"

"Well, let's start with the second questions first. Michael gets to go home because his burns were not as serious as yours were. He'll still have to come back to the hospital. He'll have to have a couple of surgeries to fix his scars. You on the other hand are going to be here for a while. I know the doctor tried to explain it to you. I'll be here with you to help you through the tough parts. Now to your first question, I think Michael thinks of you like his little sister now, and it hurts him to tell you he has to leave you here. He feels like he can't protect you if he's not here. He's just very sad.

"Oh, I get it. Trina, I have another question for you."

Trina waited as Emily put her thoughts together. There was fear in her eyes. Of what, could she possibly be afraid? She had survived the fire. She pulled a chair up beside Emily's bed.

"I was just wondering why you volunteer here. Is it because you were burned? I don't see where you were burned. Did they do something to you to make the ugly burns go away?"

Ah, now she understood. She wasn't concerned with the reason Trina volunteered. She was worried about the scarring.

"I was in an accident and was burned. They did many procedures to help me. For a long time I was afraid my friends would laugh or make fun of me because of my scars."

Surprise and relief spread across Emily's face. She knew she could ask Trina her question and not be afraid she would laugh at her.

"Trina, are they going to make fun of me?"

"Some of them may. They're not necessarily making fun of you. They feel uncomfortable when they see people like us.

They don't know what to do so they might stare, or ask questions or just make rude comments. You've been through some of the worst pain you'll ever go through. Nevertheless, words hurt also, and if you try to understand the actual reason then they don't hurt so much. Most people say things because they don't understand or they are afraid."

Puzzled Emily asked, "What would they be afraid of? I'm the one with the burns and scars."

A smile crossed her face as she answered, "Yes you are the one with the burns and scars. It doesn't matter, these people are afraid they might hurt your feelings by saying the wrong thing. They're afraid to look at you because you might think they're staring and then they won't know what to say. They get nervous and some crack jokes and some just flat out ask you about your burns. Be honest with them. They'll feel strange and uncomfortable around you for a while. Once they get to know you or are comfortable with your situation then they'll feel more comfortable around you."

Trina promised to come back later on while the nurses changed her bandages. She left Emily and went to Michael's room. She could see something was bothering him.

"I have some questions for you. I don't know if you'll even want to answer my questions because they're very personal. Were you scared when you were in the car accident and it caught on fire?"

"I was lucky that I had passed out before too much of the fire had reached me. When I flew out of the car and it landed on me, I was terrified. I couldn't breathe. When I woke up in the hospital and realized how bad I was hurt, I was afraid I'd die. I kept thinking I was too young. However, I have a feeling that's not the question you really wanted to ask, is it?"

Timidly he shook his head. "Do you have nightmares about being in the towers?"

Trina knew he would eventually get to this question. He wasn't one of the curious people wanting to know what it had

119

been like for her. She feared it had something to do with his situation. It was best to let him talk. "I have them almost every night. Sometimes they are extremely vivid and I'm not sure if I am awake or dreaming. I wake up in a cold sweat. Sometimes I wake up feeling like I can't breathe."

"What scared you the most?"

"At first, I guess I was afraid that I would burn to death because I could smell the fuel. I remembered seeing those people run past me from the elevator on fire. I could hear their screams and smell their burning flesh. I can't get that out of my head. Next, I was afraid I wouldn't see my parents again. Finally, I was afraid I'd never see my friend, who was in the other tower. Mark and I were in one tower and Lucas was in the other tower. But that still isn't the question you want to ask me is it?"

"No. How do you handle the nightmares? Everyone thinks I'm a hero. I could see Emily trying to get the window open and the flames were behind her. I could hear her screaming. Everyone just stood around saying she was going to die before the fire department got there. They did nothing except literally turn their back on her so they wouldn't have to see her die. I could hear her parents in the street screaming for someone to get their baby. I just reacted. When we were on the ground outside, I could hear her crying. They were spraying water on us to cool us down. That's when I got scared. Then it hit me how close I came to dying. I keep thinking about what the firefighter told me about being so stupid. I feel guilty because a part of me agrees with him. In my nightmares, Emily is in the house screaming my name, and I just stand there and watch her burn up. The dreams are never about me dying. They are always about me watching her die. I'm afraid that I'm a coward."

"No you are not!" said a voice behind Trina.

"Mark, I didn't know you were here." She looked at him and wondered why he had come to the hospital.

"I came by to see you and they told me you were here." He looked at the young man sitting on his bed. "You must be

Michael. Trina has told me a lot about you. I'm Mark and I want to say that I'm extremely pleased to finally meet you. Don't you ever think you are a coward because of your nightmares? The people who stood next to you and did nothing, are not necessarily cowards because they did nothing. Everyone has his or her own reasons for doing, or not doing something. The dreams are not real. I can tell you from experience that they feel just as real as you feel, sitting on that bed. Did Trina tell you that I lost my parents in a fire?"

Michael shook his head and Mark continued. "I accidentally started a fire in my bedroom while working on a model. I dozed off. My parents were already asleep. They were deaf and couldn't hear the smoke detector. When I got out through my window, I couldn't get back in to them. The neighbors held me back to keep me from running back into the house. I kept having nightmares that I killed them because I couldn't get back in the house and save them.

We do what we have to do to survive. We also do what our gut tells us. Your parents probably hope you'll never do what you did, again. Not because they think it's stupid, but because they have fears of losing you. They can't take your pain away. It hurts them and they feel guilty on their own for not being there to try to help the little girl. I know. I've talked to them. They kept telling me that if they had been home instead of at the theater, they might have heard her screams and they could have helped. Emily's parents hope that if the situation ever happened again that you, or someone as brave as you would be there to rescue her again. The nightmares won't last forever. They have to run their course. It is the way your mind is trying to make sense of all that you've been through. Talking to the counselor here will help. Holding your fears inside won't. I know I tried that. You need to talk with a professional and tell them in detail about your experience and your nightmares. They will help you deal with what you were experiencing, before you went in and after you came out. You haven't really dealt with any of it.

You've hidden feelings your mind isn't ready to handle. When it is, then the nightmares will stop. Don't confuse the nightmares ending with forgetting. This is an event you will never forget, the pain you will."

Michael's shoulders began to gently shake as tears streamed down his face. One look at his face and the relief was evident. It was as if someone had given him permission to acknowledge his feelings, no matter what his feelings were. They didn't make him the person he was. His actions showed what kind of person he was.

Mark and Trina said their goodbyes to Michael and wished him luck as they left his room. Mark stopped and looked at Trina, "You free for dinner? I have something to discuss with you."

Hesitantly she replied, "Sure, as soon as Emily has her bandages changed. I told her I'd be there for her. Why don't you wait in the lobby and I'll meet you there."

Mark agreed and kissed her lightly on the cheek. He hurried away and Trina wondered what could be so important that he had to discuss it with her over dinner.

# 17 Opportunity and Decisions

Mark and Trina picked a quiet pizza place. He wanted it to be comfortable. He chose a place that was not too noisy, and not too quiet. The place was not very full. The theaters had not yet let out, so they were guaranteed at least an hour of uninterrupted time. He sat quietly eating his first slice of pizza trying to decide how to bring up the subject. Trina could feel the tension in the air. Was he going to dump her? They had been dating since Mark had been released from the hospital. She put her pizza down and looked at him, afraid of what he would say.

"Just spill it! I can handle anything you have to say, but don't keep me in suspense." She surprised herself with the realization of how sharp her words sounded.

Mark looked at her and swallowed the lump that had formed in his throat. "I finished my fifteen hours and my first responder test." He paused and waited for an answer. He was surprised when she started to giggle. He looked at her puzzled. "Why do you find that so funny?"

She shook her head as she answered. "You looked so serious when you were at the hospital that I thought you were getting ready to dump me. I've set here unable to eat a bite wondering what you were going to say."

He was shocked. How could she have thought such a thing? He pulled her to him and planted a kiss in the middle of her forehead. "I have no intentions of dumping you, and if I had it definitely wouldn't have been like this. I wanted to talk with you because there's much more to tell than just me passing the test. I've been accepted to the Fire Academy." He held up his hands as if to stay any objections she might have. "I know your thoughts on fires and fighting fires. We've had this conversation many times before. I would never think to try to stop you from working with burn patients. We've both been through so much when it comes to disasters and fires. I've always thought I would work in a fancy office like the one Mr. Morrow had. My parents always wanted me to be successful. They would have continued to love me no matter what I did. So much has changed since that day in Mr. Morrow's office. I walked into his office, and saw all of the luxury and the view from the top and knew that I had to have what he had. Then I saw the plane rocketing toward us. As we were making our way out, and before I found you, I suddenly realized that surviving was more important than having an expensive office with a view. I feel the need and the desire to become a firefighter."

Mark could see the flash of fear in Trina's eyes. He knew what she was thinking. She was remembering all of the firefighters they had passed in the stairwell, who never made it out of the building. They never had a chance. Their faces were permanently etched into their memory. He sat and watched her as she tried to find the right words.

"I guess trying to talk you out of this would be useless. You already know my fears. You can't make your decisions based on my fears. I'll support your decision no matter what. Just know up front that this doesn't mean I have to like this. I'll constantly worry about you. I'm not afraid of you dying. My fear is that you might once again suffer burns. I just don't know if I can stand watching you go through that pain again. As a firefighter, you stand a better chance, a more realistic chance, of burning.

Mark couldn't argue that point so he tried something else. "I agree it ups the ante, but remember you were burned in a car fire, Emily was burned in a house fire. If it wasn't for fire fighters people like you and Emily might have died."

She knew that he was right and she hated it. She put a smile on her face, batted her eyes at him and said, "I guess that I'll just have to believe in you and your ability. After all you've survived a burning house, and a collapsing tower."

Mark slipped her a small smile then looked back down at his pizza. Trina saw the wrinkled brow and knew that he had more to tell her. She waited patiently. Mark put his slice of pizza down and looked at Trina. "I got a call from Lucas today."

Lucas had fought long and hard to make his father understand how much he wanted to be a teacher. He worked to keep his body physically fit, especially after surviving the collapse of both towers. His injuries had not been as serious as Mark's. He worked to get his mind and body back in shape.

His father had changed a lot since the September that changed everything. He had helped him look into the best teaching colleges. He had already completed two years at the local junior college. He and his father had spent Christmas break after 9/11 turning his apartment into a dance studio for his mother. He had never seen her so happy. For the first time in a long time, his mother and father looked like they were falling in love again. His relationship with his father had changed as well. They spent less and less time at the country club. His father's old friends just didn't seem to understand his decision to let his son become a teacher, or his decision to let his wife put her former dance skills to use. They were afraid their wives might get the same idea about what they called frivolous work. Mark really didn't see that happening. The main difference between his father, and the other men at the country club was simple. His father had worked hard to earn every penny he had, and the other men had inherited theirs. There had been other changes between he and his father after 9/11. He and his father still fought on occasion. The difference was, they were both willing to sit down and discuss the situation like men and come to a decision.

Lucas sat in his car trying to garner the courage to enter the house and talk with his parents. For the first time he had made a decision and executed it without talking it over with his mother and father first. He wasn't sure how his parents were going to handle it. He ran his hands through his hair and chuckled. He would not have a hair problem much longer. He opened the car door and stepped out. He gave himself one more pep talk and then shut the door and headed for the house.

As Lucas entered the house, he called out to his parents.

"We're in the den Lucas", called his father.

He could hear his mother giggling. He wondered what was so funny. He entered and saw that they were watching a video. His mother had video-taped her class at their first rehearsal for their first performance. She was laughing at a child of not more than four years old. Her name was Amy. Her animated dancing brought laughter to all. His mother had seemed to fall in love with this girl the minute she had met her. This class was extra special to her. After his mother had opened her studio, she visited the homes of several families who had lost a loved one in the Towers. She offered a special class free or at reduced rates to them. It was a part of the healing process for all of them. She had an area where they could sit and drink coffee, have a snack, and bond while their children danced. Amy was one of those special children. She had lost both parents in the towers. Amy lived with her grandparents. Dancing gave them a bit of a breather each afternoon. Amy had captured his mother's heart the first time they had met. His mother asked her why she wanted to learn to dance. Amy's reply brought a gasp and tears from the adults.

"I want to dance for my mommy and daddy in heaven so they'll be happy. That way they'll know I'm happy." She'd said this so matter-of-factly. Amy danced her heart out. When her over-enthusiasm got a giggle out of people she smiled because she loved making people happy.

Lucas' father had noticed this charitable attitude and offered a similar thing for the boys. He offered golfing lessons and tennis lessons. He paid for the best instructors for these children. It was his way of giving back. Since his country club refused to allow these non-members in, he had started his own club with the help of several of his new friends and new law partners. They paid for tee times and court times at some of the local golf courses and tennis clubs. He even provided a van to pick up those who had no ride. The van had been Lucas' donation. It was funny how much a tragedy could bring unknown people together.

Lucas sat quietly on the couch until the video was over. His dad continued to giggle as he turned off the video. One look at Lucas and his father stopped giggling. "Is something wrong?"

Lucas took a deep breath. "No, nothing is wrong. However, I did something today without talking to you first about it. I want you to hear me out before you start yelling."

Lucas watched the face of his parents change. They knew that what he had to tell them was serious, especially if he was concerned about not telling them first. Today I went to the local recruiter's office and signed up."

"You what?" his father boomed. "Don't you think you should have talked to us about this first?"

"Actually, I don't", he replied calmly. Lucas looked his father straight in the eye. I've been thinking about this a lot. You and I both know from what we have been hearing on the news that they need more men to fight this war on terror. They started it by flying those planes into the towers and the Pentagon. You've been great about supporting me, so let me finish. Since I came out of those towers, I felt I should do more with my life. I feel it deep down in my soul that I need to enlist to support my country. Before you go giving me a lecture dad, remember, you were once in the military. You used to tell me how much it built your character and made you the man you are today."

Lucas' father closed his mouth. His mother sat with a terrified look on her face. "But Lucas, you could be killed."

Lucas loved his mother, she never minced words. "Yes, mother. While crossing the street, a car could hit me. I almost died just by visiting a high rise. At least I feel like I am in charge of my destiny by entering the Army. When I was in the Towers, I had no control. It was up to me to get myself out, but I could only go so fast. At least in the Army, I can say I knew what to expect when I signed up. It was my choice. I also knew if I came and asked you first you would try to talk me out of it. I've already taken the ASVAB and signed up."

Suddenly his mother burst into tears. "I am so proud of you. You've grown so much. You are the most awesome young man I know." She jumped up and grabbed Lucas, crushing him to her in a bear hug. His father stood and clapped him on the back and joined in the hug. Lucas was stunned. He had not expected this reaction from them. He sat with his parents and explained what had happened that day at the recruiter's office.

That conversation seemed to have happened years ago, when in fact, it had been just a little under a year. Here he was at Fort Drum. In his opinion, he was with one of the best units available. He loved the physical part of being in the Army. He was proud to serve his country. He felt this was something he had to do. Now he had to get ready to leave because he was being deployed. He felt a mixture of emotions; pride for serving his country and fear because he would face the unknown. He would do whatever it took to come back to his family and his country in one piece. He put those thoughts out of his mind and headed across base for final instructions. He would have one of his buddies mail the letters to his family and friends after he was gone.

# 18  The Letter

Trina stared at the letter in her hands.  She had already called Mark and asked him to meet her after work.  He was exhausted.  He had just finished a twelve-hour shift.  Still, Trina seemed extremely upset.  Could it be one of her young patients had died?  It seemed like they saw very little of each other any more.  If she was not at school, or at the hospital, then she was home studying.  She was working so hard to finish her studies.  She was on a fast track and had only six more months before she would complete enough courses to take her state test.  Once she passed it, she would have her nursing license.   She was determined to put in another year to work full time in the burn department as a specialist.  Her strong background in math and chemistry had allowed her to test out of several classes.  That is what Eagle Prep did for its students, gave them an academic edge.

Mark parked in the parking garage then walked the three blocks to Trina's apartment.  He knocked on the door and waited.  When Trina finally opened the door, he was alarmed.  Her red eyes and runny nose told him she had been crying.  This must have been a hard case.  She usually held it together unless it was a baby.  Even he hated the calls where a baby was involved.  They were the most innocent victims.  He followed Trina into the living room and sat on the couch next to her. He pulled her next to him and held her until she could collect herself. He looked around him.  He liked being in her apartment.  It was a cozy feeling.  She had taken little from her family home when she moved into her apartment.   She figured it was just a stepping- stone along her path.  She did not need a lot of clutter.  He looked at the bookcase filled with her nursing books.  She had charts hanging on her walls.  There was no television.  She said she wanted to remain focused on her studies.  She had a radio set to her local classical station.  She had told him if there was anything important she needed to know, someone would inform her. Her couch also served as her fold out bed. Along one wall was a desk. It was simple, just like her. Unlike his family, Trina's parents had money. They lived in one of the nicest houses he had ever been in. It seemed so funny that she wanted the opposite. He often thought of her as a modern day Mother Teresa. She was always taking care of others. Often she forgot to take care of herself.

Before he could take off his coat, Trina once again buried her face in his jacket and sobbed. He said nothing to her as he gently stroked her hair. He let her cry herself out before asking what had happened. Instead of speaking, she handed him an envelope. It was evident from its rumpled appearance that she had opened it, and read it many times.

"Read it", she told him.

Mark opened the letter and began to read.

*Dear Trina and Mark,*

*I just wanted to let you know that I'll soon be in Afghanistan. I'll send you more information later. For now, I want you to know that I'm safe. I was unable to tell you, the last time we had talked, that I was deploying. I knew that I was going but was under strict orders to tell no one. It's a matter of national security that they don't let us tell our parents or loved ones the time and origin of our departure. We won't know where we're headed until the day we leave. As you know, security is very tight right now. We're on high alert. I know you're shocked to get this news. Mark, give Trina a hug right now for me. I know she needs it. Tell her to stop crying because I'll be okay. I figure it this way. I survived a crash that I caused and that injured Trina; then I survived the collapse of not one but two towers, so this should be a walk in the park. No, I am not naïve enough to believe that this war is a walk in the park, but I do need to keep my morale up. I have a favor to ask you both. Please call and visit my parents. I've sent them a similar letter and I know my mother will worry. If she sees you two and you can convince her that I'm okay, she'll not worry as much. I appreciate it, and will send you updates. I love you both. Trina, I know I don't need to ask you to keep up the prayers. Your faith has helped carry me through when things got tough. I want to say thank you to both of you. I love you and will write again soon. When I do, I'll give you the address to write back to me. Mark, you really need to talk with Trina about the source of her strength. I love you guys.*

*Lucas*

Mark looked at Trina's tear-stained face. "I had no idea he was being deployed. I knew that he was stationed at Fort Drum. I've had so little time to write to him, I don't even know what his job is."

Trina's voice shook as she asked, "Do you think he'll be okay Mark?"

"I'm sure he will. He has more lives than a cat. I think we need to visit his parents this evening. Shall I call them or do you want to?"

"You go ahead and call them. I'm afraid if I do they'll get the wrong idea and think something has happened to Lucas."

Mark called Lucas' parents and set up a time to meet with them. He turned back to Trina who looked exhausted. "Go lay down and take a nap. I'll go home and shower and come back for you. Give me your key and I'll let myself in and wake you in about an hour and then we can visit his parents."

Trina reluctantly shuffled off to the bedroom. He could hear her sniffling and knew she was taking this hard. His concern was that she still had feelings for Lucas. Mark chastised himself thinking about how silly it was that he was jealous of Lucas. First, he and Trina had been together since he had gotten out of the hospital. Second, she and Lucas were just friends and he would soon be out of the country. He hated when he read more into the situation than was there. He locked the apartment door and drove home. As he entered his apartment, he reached for the phone. He first called Trina's parents and then he called his parents. He let them know about Lucas' letter. He informed both of them that he and Trina would be heading over to Lucas' parents house to be with them as they read their letter. He quickly showered and returned to pick up Trina.

An hour and a half later, they pulled into the James' driveway. Mrs. James greeted them.

"Mark, Trina, come on in."

They followed her into the house. Mr. James entered from the kitchen with some coffee. The four of them sat down in the living room. Trina saw the envelope on the table. It hadn't been opened yet. Mrs. James looked at the letter.

"It came in a manila envelope today and there was a note inside with the envelope that asked us to wait until you and Mark were here to open it. Do you know what this is about?"

Mark nodded, unable to get the words to come out. Mr. James picked up the envelope, slit the edge and began to read aloud.

*Dear Mom and Dad,*

*I know this will come as a shock to you so I've asked Trina and Mark to be there with you. This letter is to let you know that I've received my orders for deployment. I don't want you to worry too much about me. You know that I'm safe and in God's hands. Trina and Mark are there for support. They love you as much as I do. If you need anything, just talk with them. I love you both.*

*Lucas*

The silence was so thick in the room you could have cut it with a knife. Trina took one look at Mrs. James and ran to her, throwing her arms around her in a hug. The two of them shook as they cried. Mr. James continued to read the letter over, and over again as if reading it again would change things.

Mr. James cleared his throat, "Mark, did you and Trina know about this?"

"No sir. Trina received a letter just like yours today. I'm sure that he'll be okay over there. Besides he had to go through mobilization before they sent him over."

Mr. James nodded his head. Mark and Trina stayed and talked a while longer then Mark dropped her off at her apartment. Sleep didn't come easy to any of them that night. For Mark and Trina it triggered nightmares they had not had for a long time.

# 19 Mobilization

Lucas loved being in the Army. He loved the physicality and the work ethic. He knew that what he learned now would be some of the most important things he could ever learn. This would prepare him for his deployment to Afghanistan. He knew when he signed up that he would most likely be deployed, yet he signed on the dotted line. He felt a strong desire to right the wrongs committed against American on 9/11. He had been advised that this would be the toughest two and a half months of his life, and they were not kidding. Some of the things he did and learned for mobilization, he found boring, as did most of the men. He knew all of it was important especially as they were preparing to deploy.

He and the other men in his unit, had sat through hours of combined power point presentations and field trainings. These presentations covered everything from the rules of engagement, the escalation of force, to the use of force.

He paid special attention to his field training. He knew this training could mean the difference between life, or death. His days had been filled with the typical weapons training and qualifications, traffic control points, how and when to stop and search a car, and entry control points. They had to learn the standard operating procedures for everything. It seemed as everything had a standard operating procedure. There was so much to learn. Most important was the training for dealing with IEDs or Improvised Explosive Devices. The insurgents were constantly making them out of whatever they had on hand. They used pipes, glass, clay, nails. They resembled pipe bombs but with much more deadly consequences. They were made to do as much damage as possible. They trained for different scenarios. They had to learn how to react to contact with the enemy, as well as how to react to the locals. They needed to learn how to react to an ambush. Learning all about Medi-vac procedures was just as important a safety issue as learning battle strategies. Each of them had gunner training and of course, drivers training.

The thing Lucas found most difficult was getting used to all of the men and their different personalities. He was cooped up with a large number of men all day long. With that many men in such close quarters there were always arguments, yelling and wrestling matches. This was to be expected. They were housed in a long building with four separate wings. These buildings held between forty and fifty men. They contained six sinks, three urinals, six toilets and eight showers. To him they constantly stank and appeared dirty. He figured this was to be expected since there were so many men.

One thing he would never get used to, was all of the shots and paperwork. The shots were vaccines for Hepatitis A, B, and C, Anthrax, the flu, and smallpox. They felt ill for days afterwards. Some of the men became real sick. If the shots didn't kill you, then you were bored to death with all of the paperwork.

He and the other men in his unit trained in full gear. His battle Kevlar weighed eight pounds and he carried one hundred eighty rounds of 5.56 mm ammo. They also carried a first aid kit. All of this weighed sixty to sixty five pounds. Add to that weight the seven and a half pound M-4 weapon and the five pound camel back, a three gallon bladder with a capped rubber hose that carried his precious water, and you had quite a bit of weight before adding anything else to it. His assault pack added twenty to forty pounds. It contained food water, ammo, and a spare set of clothes. They trained in all of this gear so they would be used to it. They trained in all types of weather. He knew the weather in Afghanistan was usually either extremely hot, or bitterly cold. He was determined to be as prepared for any situation so that he and his buddies could return home safely.

He learned very quickly that it was not real popular to talk about God. One of his Christian buddies, Ron, did nothing but preach to them or at them. The men no longer knew if he would have their backs when it came to a fire-fight. He relied on his faith to carry him but was afraid to talk about it much. He knew that no matter what, if it came down to taking a life or his life being taken he could take the kill shot.

Ron was constantly talking about how much they needed to love these people and try to find a different way to get through to them. He didn't think war was the way to go about it. It was for this reason the men didn't trust him. If it came down to him killing or letting one of them be killed, could he do it?

Lucas noticed a lot of the men had changed from the time he first met them. A lot of them talked about their faith and read their Bible regularly. After a while it seemed like this was replaced with drinking, dirty jokes and lewd remarks about women. Lucas didn't gush about his religious beliefs but he held true to them. The men knew they could count on him.

He continued his training awaiting the day they would all send off the letter letting their loved ones know they would be leaving. Some of them would take a leave to see their wife or children without telling them they were going. Other men and women. like Lucas, chose to send a letter. It almost seemed cowardly. He just didn't want to face them and see the hurt, fear, and anxiety in their faces. He knew he could not stand to see Trina's face. She had always worried about him. It would be easier just to know she was praying for him daily. It was also easier, knowing she had Mark.

It seemed funny that he had just received an email from Mark. Mark had something to discuss with him and needed his input on the matter. They had come a long way in their relationship. It was strange to think they had met underneath the Towers and the events of that day had made them friends. Mark was the type of true friend he had been looking for all his life.

None of the men in his unit knew that he came from money at all. He had shared very little about his private life. They knew he was one of the lucky ones to survive the Towers and that seemed to earn him a little more respect. They honored his privacy. They refused to ask him about those days. They all assumed, rightly so, that those events were what led Lucas to join the Army.

There was no way that Lucas could ever explain to them the events of that day. Most of them had watched it unfold on their television sets. None of them had really known what it was like. None of them could comprehend the despair you felt knowing some of the people who lost their lives on that day. None of them could ever feel the anger he felt at having survived when others did not. That was the reason he was here. He was here, to avenge and set right what had happened. He was here, to honor those who had lost their lives on that day. He was angry, but he refused to hate these people. Hatred would lower him to their level, and he didn't want to stoop that low. He had prayed for God to show him how to love the people of this country. He knew the Bible said to love your enemy. That did not mean he was not to protect those who could not protect themselves. He knew what he was getting into and he did his job to the best of his ability. He took the training exercises to prepare him to deploy seriously. He was the best that he could be.

# 20 Rules of Engagement

Mark nervously paced back and forth in Dr. Lacy's home office. Just two days earlier he had called Dr. Lacy and scheduled an appointment with him. He had an urgent matter on his mind. He needed to discuss it with Trina's father before he discussed it with her. Mrs. Lacy entered the room with a tray containing two cups of coffee and placed it on the table in front of the couch. She smiled reassuringly at Mark. She had an idea why he was there and sympathized with him. She remembered when her husband had paid just such a visit to her father. She could only hope that her husband was as sensitive and understanding as her father had been with her husband. She smiled at her husband as he entered, and she quickly closed the door.

"Mark, so good to see you. Please have a seat." Dr. Lacy gestured to a chair on the other side of the table, across from him. Mark sat wringing his hands and bouncing his right knee up and down. "So what brings you here to speak with me today?" he asked with a twinkle in his eye.

"Sir, you know Trina and I have been together ever since I got out of the hospital. I believe you know how much I love your daughter. I came today to ask your permission to marry Trina."

"Have you talked with Trina about this?"

"No sir, I figured it would be best to get your permission first." Mark clasped his hands together and waited for an answer."

"Mark you know I like you very much." Mark cringed waiting for a negative answer. "You've been very good for Trina. That is one thing, of which I'm sure. Before I give you my answer I'd like to ask my wife to join us. After all this question you have asked involves us both." Dr. Lacy walked across the room and into the hall. He knew his wife would not be far away. As he led her into his office Mark began to sweat. What if they told him no, because he didn't have much money?

His mind ran from one possible scenario to the next. Mrs. Lacy took a chair next to her husband's chair.

"Mark has asked permission to marry our daughter. He claims to love her very much. He has not yet discussed this matter with Trina, so I'm not sure how she feels about Mark." He watched Mark squirm just a bit more. "I told him that this was a question that you must weigh in on as Trina's mother. Can you think of any reason why we should deny this young man permission to marry our daughter?" Mrs. Lacy tried to hold the giggle inside. She was aware her husband was making Mark squirm the way her father had made him squirm.

"Why no, I can think of no reason. He's a loving and respectable boy. He's always had Trina's best interest at heart, and I do believe he loves her very much. I'd give him my permission and blessing, but what about you?" Dr. Lacy looked at Mark as if he was trying to figure out how worthy the boy was of his daughter. The look had the desired effect. Both of Mark's knees were now bouncing up and down. It was time to let him off the hook. "Mark my boy, welcome to the family. You have not only our permission but our blessings."

Mark blew out a sign of relief. This had been the hardest thing he had ever had to do in his entire life. He was relieved it was over. Surely asking Trina would be easier. He looked up as Dr. and Mrs. Lacy began to stand and saw Dr. Lacy shaking all over with laughter.

"Mark I am so sorry to have put you through that. I was pretty sure when you called to set up a meeting with me what this was all about. After my wife's father put me through the wringer like this, I swore if we ever had a daughter I would never do this to her boyfriend. When I walked in and saw how nervous you were, I just couldn't help myself." By now, the tears were running down his face from laughing so hard. The bubble of tension that had filled the room had burst. Now all three of them were laughing and hugging.

"Sir I want you to know, if Trina accepts my proposal, I'll do everything in my power to make her happy and keep her safe."

Dr. Lacy nodded. He knew the bond had been sealed between his daughter and Mark, the day he had laid his life on the line for her. His hope was that he would receive a call from his daughter later on that evening with the good news that she had accepted his proposal.

Mark thanked her parents and left. He had scheduled a dinner date with Trina. Mark knew that most men would take their girlfriends to a real fancy and expensive restaurant and then pop the question. He did not really want to give it away, so he had told her he was in the mood to do something fun. They often ate at Ellen's Stardust Diner. It was fun to be served food from the fifties while being serenaded by waitresses and waiters. Often they would go to the theater before or after going to the diner. As a firefighter his budget was limited so he wanted to save as much money as he could for the wedding. He put on a pair of jeans and a sweater over his t-shirt. It didn't matter that it was summer. In Manhattan, the temperatures could drop quickly at night. He drove the few blocks to Trina's apartment to pick her up.

"So what did you have planned this evening for fun?"

"Well, I thought we would eat at Ellen's Stardust Diner and then visit the Empire State Building. You know I've never been to the top of that building?"

"You're kidding me right? You've never been to the top of the Empire State Building?"

"Nope! I thought tonight would be the perfect night. It is not too hot or too cold. I would bring a sweater or jacket because you know how fast the temperature can drop. I just figured I wanted to do something I'd never done before and I wanted to experience it with you."

"Aw Mark, that is so sweet. Are you sure you are okay with the height of the building? I mean I remember how long it took me to go into a building that was taller than five stories, after the

Towers collapsed. I felt like I was suffocating. I kept looking for the exit and the stairs just in case."

Mark smiled, understanding exactly what she was talking about. "I'm fine. The training I've gone through with the fire department helped with that. I am fine. I've never been to the top of the Empire State Building so I won't be able to say until I'm up there. I do promise I won't flip out on you."

Trina laughed and grabbed her jacket. They found a parking garage not too far from the theater district and decided to walk to the diner. The crowd was manageable as they entered. Once the theaters began to let out there would be no room. They were shown to a booth where they both ordered their favorite foods.

They both ordered a bowl of hot chicken soup, figuring it would warm them up. There was already a slight nip in the air. Trina ordered her usual veggie burger topped with grilled portobella mushrooms. Mark ordered an eight-ounce burger with Portobello mushrooms and jack cheese. He knew what was coming next and he waited.

"Mark, think of all the fat in that burger. One day you have got to try the veggie burger. It is so much healthier for you." Mark looked at Trina, grinned and took a big bite from his burger making sure he smacked his lips to let her know how good it was. She just laughed. As soon as they had finished, they paid and left. They walked to the Empire State Building and entered another world.

The entrance to the Empire State Building was grand. There was marble and gold everywhere. It was one of the most opulent places Mark had ever seen. They paid and headed for the first set of elevators. Once they had reached the eighty-sixth floor Mark took Trina's hand and led her onto the observation deck. It was nice here. There was a saxophonist playing mood music. It was very romantic. Mark was tempted to pop the question there but decided not to. As they turned to leave, they observed a young man drop to his knee and propose to a very surprised date. Trina let out a sigh, "That is so romantic."

Mark looked at them and then at Trina and shrugged it off.

"Yeah, I guess so." He led her back into the building and to the bank of elevators. When the elevator stopped at the 102$^{nd}$ floor they stepped out of the west door. They walked to the wall and gazed out at the night view. They stood silently taking in the sight. They re-entered and exited the north and the East sides of the building taking in the different views. As they prepared to walk out the door of the south side of the building Mark took Trina's hand. They walked to the wall and looked out. There was an empty area where the Towers once stood. Mark and Trina both felt overcome with emotion. He hugged her tight. Slowly he let one hand slip into his pants pocket and remove the ring box. As he released Trina from the hug he quickly dropped to one knee.

"Trina Lacy would you consider being my wife?" With that said, he opened the ring box and held it out to her. For the first time in her life she was totally speechless. The silence was so long that Mark was afraid she was going to say no.

"She screeched out a "Yes" as she threw her arms around Marks neck and kissed him. Those standing around who had witnessed this wonderful event applauded the young couple. Mark took the ring from the box and slid it onto her finger. He watched the tears slide down her cheeks.

"I can't wait to tell my parents."

"Oh, don't worry, they know and they will be waiting for your call."

"What do you mean my parents know?"

"I paid a visit to your parents this afternoon and asked their permission to marry you."

Trina was thrilled that Mark thought so much of her family that he would ask her father's permission. It really meant a lot to her. "I know someone we haven't told."

Mark looked at Trina, trying to figure out what she was thinking. "I emailed Lucas and let him know I was going to propose. I hope you don't mind."

Trina shook her head. At that point, she felt a little conflicted. She loved Mark with all of her heart but a part of her had wanted to tell Lucas herself. It would have been the final closure in their relationship, and she needed closure. She would have to talk with him at some point. She put those thoughts out of her mind and thought, "in a few months, I will be known as Trina Jacobs." She could not wait to call her mom and dad that evening and tell them everything that had happened. Tomorrow would be a new day for her at work. She could hardly wait to show off the ring. It was a simple ring with a center diamond flanked by two smaller diamonds on each side, set in white gold. She had never seen a more beautiful ring in her life. She knew when the evening was over she would have wonderful dreams as she drifted off to sleep.

# 21 Final Letters

*Mark and Trina,*

*First, let me say congratulations to the two of you. You both deserve this happiness. You will find this letter short as I need to write one more before going off on patrol, or as we call it around here, 'into the belly of the beast'. Trina, we've been friends for so long that I need to say something to ease your mind. I know you probably wanted to talk with me to make sure I was okay with this situation. If I hadn't been okay with it, I would have tried to get back with you a long time ago. We had something very special. The accident ripped that from us. I was determined to win back our friendship. When you and Mark went on your first date, I knew then that the two of you were meant to be. I am so happy for you both.*

*Mark, thanks for asking me to be your best man. I accept the offer and look forward to that day. Let me know when the date is. I only have a month left on this tour and then I'll be home. I look forward to hooking up with you when I return. Until then, I send you both my love.*

*Lucas*

Lucas took out another sheet of paper. He had one final letter to write. He decided he needed to get it done. It had been pressing on him for quite some time.

*To My Family and Friends,*

*As I sit here preparing to go on patrol, death surrounds me and I feel it closer every day. I realize each morning as I awake that this could be my last day. Today this presses on me even more. I don't know why. For this reason, I felt I needed to put some things into writing, hoping you never have to receive this letter.*

*Since the day I walked down those tower stairs, I've felt that I needed to do something to stop these terrorists. In my heart, I know I made the right decision by joining the Army. If I can help prevent the loss of life of a few people here, and prevent the terrorists from reaching our soil again, then I would gladly lay down my life. I've seen so much here. One minute you're on patrol and a child or old woman walking to get water is blown up by an IED. I've also experienced happiness. The little things, such as teddy bears and candy can brighten the eyes of a child who has learned to trust no one. Their life expectancy is so much shorter because terrorists don't care if they kill their own people. For one moment, we're able to bring about peace and happiness.*

*I think about the men I am fighting. They are someone's son or father, and I wonder, do they think about me that way as they shoot at me? I know my enemy and sometimes I am horrified at my coldness toward them. When I kick in a door, I have to know that the other men in my squad have my back, because the enemy here doesn't wear a uniform. I must put aside all feelings because the child strapped with twenty pounds of C-4 on a suicide mission must be taken out if I am to save myself and my men. Yes, it does happen. I often feel as if I have become a different person. I find myself at times to be cold, rude and mean. I must be willing to do what needs to be done, for what I and the other men here think is right. We in the infantry are rough, tough, down and dirty. We like to get in the mix of things. We can go from making fun of each other one minute to taking a bullet for that same guy the next. I'm still me inside, just tougher on the outside. Please know that I love you. My life here is in God's hands and I accept with no trepidation what he has in store for me here or at home.*

*Love to all,*

*Lucas*

# 22 Notification

Mark and Trina sat in the living room with Mr. and Mrs. James. The tears flowed freely in the room. The letter sat on the table like a cancer. The hole it created was so deep that Trina felt like she may tumble into its darkness forever. The letter had been delivered just an hour earlier. It simply stated Lucas had been injured in an IED explosion while on patrol. He was being flown to Landstuhl Regional Medical Center in Germany. The soldier who had delivered the letter had told them to wait for further information. He left them a contact number where they would be able to find out more about Lucas' condition, and when he would arrive on American soil.

Mrs. James rocked back and forth on the sofa. It was 9/11 all over again. They had to sit and wait without knowing how their son was. She hated the helpless feeling. She looked over at Trina and saw her with her head bowed. She knew she was upset, yet a peace seemed to flow from her. She knew at that moment that the only thing she had to hold onto was her own faith and so she too bowed her head and prayed not only for her son, but for the other young men in his unit and their parents who were going through the same thing they were experiencing.

Mark and Trina left Lucas' parents with their pastor and headed to the home of Trina's parents. Trina entered the house calling out for her parents. Her father entered the room and Trina ran into his arms.

"Trina, what's the matter? You're shaking all over." Mark came in behind her and looked at his future father-in-law.

"Sir, we've just come from the James' home. A letter was delivered to them a little over an hour ago. Lucas has been injured in combat."

Dr. Lacy led Trina to a couch. "Honey, I'm sure he'll be okay. What did the letter say?"

Trina wiped her eyes with a tissue and tried to collect herself. "They said he was flown to a hospital in Germany and we'll have to wait until they let us know when he's transferred to the United States. I don't even know how bad he is."

"Do you remember the name of the hospital in Germany? If so I might be able to call and find out something."

Trina was so upset she couldn't recall the name of the hospital. She looked pleadingly at Mark. "Do you remember?"

Mark pulled an envelope from his pocket where he had written the information down. "The name is Landstuhl Regional Medical Center. I didn't see a phone number."

"Not a problem. Let me call a friend and see what I can find out." He left his daughter and Mark sitting in the living room. Trina's mother came in with cups of coffee and some small sandwiches.

"I know food is the last thing on your mind right now but your father said to make you eat something to keep your blood sugar up." She handed a small plate to Mark. He placed a sandwich on it and handed it to Trina. She sat looking at it for a minute before taking it. She took a bite just to please her mother. She might as well have been eating cardboard. She had absolutely no taste for food. Mark sat eating his sandwich and watching Trina. He wanted to be there for her but he was afraid her emotions ran deeper than he could help her. He knew a part of her still loved Lucas and always would. He constantly fought jealousy over this.

Dr. Lacy entered the room. His face had taken on a gray hue and his wrinkled forehead told them that he had bad news for them.

"I've never sugar-coated things and I won't start now. I called a buddy of mine who is over in Landstuhl. I explained that I was Lucas' family physician, and a personal friend of his family. I asked for any information I could pass on to make the wait time a little more bearable. He said Lucas' squad had gone out to back up another squad under attack. En route, they hit a roadside bomb. Lucas was blown out of the vehicle and has severely broken bones in both legs, shrapnel injuries to his face and they're sure he suffered a traumatic brain injury. They're just not sure how severe the brain injury is. They're prepping him to fly into Walter Reed Hospital in Washington, DC tomorrow. He has given me the name of a doctor to contact at Walter Reed. I'll contact him the day after tomorrow. That will give them time to stabilize him and evaluate him to give us more information. I'm going to drive over to his parents house and talk with them. Then we'll see about me driving them to the hospital to visit Lucas. If I see him and his doctor I'll be able to give you more information. Trina, I know you understand how severe a brain injury can be, but I don't want you to jump to any conclusions. It may just be a very severe concussion."

For the first time in years, Trina sounded like a frightened little girl when she replied, "Okay, daddy, I'll wait to see what you have to say when you get back. I'll just keep praying that he'll be okay. Is it okay if I stay here for the next few days? Mark can drive me home to get some clothes and pick up my car."

Mrs. Lacy hugged her daughter, "Of course you can stay here. Mark, if you'd like to stay we have a guest bedroom."

"Thanks for the offer, but right now I need to take Trina home to get her things and then I'm on duty for the next twenty-four hours. I'll keep in touch. If anything happens or you get any more information please let me know."

"We will." Dr. and Mrs. Lacy hugged Trina and told her they would see her soon. They watched her and Mark walk to the car and drive off. Mrs. Lacy turned to her husband. "Now tell me what you didn't tell your daughter."

"You sure do know me well." He took his wife's hand and led her into the den. They sat looking out the window at the water. "The doctor told me that Lucas was thrown quite a distance from the vehicle. From what they've been able to piece together a group of children saw them and came running out. The driver swerved to avoid the children and hit an IED. The driver, was killed instantly. By some miracle the blast blew Lucas' door open and he was blown free of the vehicle. Several of the children were killed as well. The gunner had just pulled himself back inside to say something to the driver when they hit the bomb. He was killed from the blast knocking his brain around like jelly inside his skull. They're worried about the brain injury because Lucas hasn't regained consciousness yet and doesn't respond to commands. They know some of the shrapnel was embedded in his skull. Until he regains consciousness they won't know if he's suffered any hearing or vision loss. He seems to be in a coma. That can be both good and bad. We'll just have to wait and see. I'm going to drive over to his parents' house. I'd like for you to come with me as support to Mrs. James."

Mrs. Lacy stood and grabbed her sweater, "I'd be glad to go with you. I can only imagine how she must feel. I remember how we waited for word on Trina and my sister. The waiting is the hardest part."

In silence, they walked to the car and headed to the home of their friends to offer what news and support they could.

# 23 The Belly of the Beast

Lucas was sitting in his tent relaxing when the call came. They were to provide backup to a squad who had come under fire. He grabbed his gear and headed with the rest of his squad to the Humvee. He prepared to take his place as gunner.

Dakota quickly shoved Lucas out of the way. "Oh no you don't. If you remember, I won the right to sit in the fresh air in the last poker game. You have the privilege of sitting in the stinky inside. You can have the small window to look out of while I take in the view from above. Besides I feel claustrophobic today."

Lucas laughed at Dakota and punched him playfully in the arm. "No problem bro. I'd rather smell your stinky boots than your stinky breath." Lucas ran around to the side of the Humvee and took his place. The rest of them quickly loaded up, and headed out of the safety of the compound. They were all on alert. On these trips there was always the possibility that they were being sent into a trap. He said a quiet prayer for those they were headed to assist. Lucas had joked with the men all morning. He had complained about being bored just sitting there doing nothing. He knew that he could only write so many letters and play so many card games. He had books to read, but on this day he just couldn't seem to get into anything. He felt restless. He had been plagued with an uneasy feeling, even though the day had passed with no problems. It had probably been one of the most boring days since he had arrived.

His mind wandered back to the first day he had arrived in Afghanistan. He was awed by how beautiful the mountains were. At the same time he could not believe how dirty and stinky the place seemed. The poverty seemed to be everywhere. He often saw children whose appearance seemed dirty or unkempt. He trusted no one except his own men. They had been warned that children were often used to set booby traps for the soldiers. After all, who would suspect a small child? Worse yet, were the children who acted as suicide bombers. He could never understand a country that valued life so little, that they would send a child, wired with C-4 to blow themselves and the soldiers up. It seemed like a coward's way to kill soldiers. Why not send an adult? Did they figure the life expectancy of a child was so slim that it was better to send a child?

Lucas heard his buddies talking about their mission. Their friends were pinned down about five miles away, and they were taking heavy fire. Lucas' team was to provide backup so that the men could safely exit the area. He had done this more times than he could count. No matter how many times he had done this he knew he could not let his guard down. The key was to stay alert. He only had a month left of his tour, and then he would be headed home. He wanted to finish his stint in the military and then continue his education to become a PE teacher. He had Mark and Trina's wedding to go to when he returned. He knew they had waited to set a permanent date because they were waiting to hear from him. It made him happy to give them that date.

He imagined how beautiful Trina would look. He could picture the love on her face for Mark. He hoped that one day he would be blessed with such a wonderful woman. If the accident had not taken Trina from him something else would have. Their relationship was not meant to be. He was not jealous of Mark. He loved Mark like a brother and would do anything for him. He knew the day he met Mark in the Mall under the Trade Centers that they would be friends. Mark seemed to see past the money his family had. He saw him for who he was. He remembered how they had planned for Mark's birthday party so he could get to know some of the other guys at school. They never did get to have that party. Maybe when he was back home they could fulfill that plan. Either way, that experience sealed their friendship forever. He, Mark and Trina had something they could share with no one else. It was a bond forged by the events of September eleventh.

Lucas was suddenly jolted back to the present. He heard the driver swear then  yell at a group of kids running toward their vehicle. They were always on the street looking for candy or food. For a minute he thought they would hit one of them. Kids like this were always hungry and took every opportunity they could to find food. It was sad that they had to beg like this. The driver swerved to miss the children running into the street. Suddenly Mark heard an ear-splitting explosion. His ear popped then had a feeling of being blocked.  He momentarily felt himself flying through the air, along with the bodies of several children, and then everything went black.

# 24 Return and Recovery

Lucas slowly opened his eyes. He wasn't sure where he was. He could not see anything. He could not move. He could hear someone appear by his side. He could hear them as they moved around checking something, before he closed his eyes and was asleep again.

Several hours had passed before Lucas opened his eyes again. When he did he was surprised to hear Dr. Lacy. He knew his eyes were open so why couldn't he see? He tried to ask a question and found it difficult to form the words.

"Hello Lucas. Welcome home."

Home? Did everyone get out of the Towers? Where was Trina and Mark? Did they make it out? His thoughts ran together. He tried to sort them out.

Dr. Lacy could see how frustrated Lucas was becoming. "Just relax Lucas. Can you hear me?"

Lucas tried once again to answer. "If you can hear me, don't try to speak, just close your eyes and open them again. Lucas followed the command. "Do you know where you are?"

Dr. Lacy could see the fear in his eyes. Lucas did not respond. "You're safe in a hospital back in the States. You've been in an explosion and were injured. You're being taken care of. If you understand what I just said then blink your eyes." Slowly Lucas closed then opened his eyes.

Why couldn't he talk? Why couldn't he move? Was he blind? Was he paralyzed? Did the Towers fall on him? How long had he been trapped? Were Mark and Trina trapped as well?

"Lucas I want you to listen to me. You have a tube down your throat to help you breathe. Relax and don't struggle against it. Until they remove it, you won't be able to talk. After they remove it you will find you will only be able to whisper at first. So just relax. You've got injuries to both legs so you can't move

153

them. You are not paralyzed. Don't panic, everything will be just fine. I'm going to go get your parents now. Don't worry if they start blubbering like idiots. Most parents act that way when they haven't seen their child in several months. I'll go get them now."

Lucas' parents entered his room. He heard his mother gasp. She leaned down to hug him and he could feel the tears flowing freely down her cheeks. She was trying to stop the tears. He could hear the concern in his father's voice and knew he, was doing a much better job of holding it together.

"Lucas honey, I'm so glad you're back here in the states. We've missed you terribly. The doctors said we could only stay a few minutes because they're going to come in and remove the tube. They said you won't be able to talk for a few days only whisper. We wanted you to know that they've put us up at one of the hotels so we'll be back to see you tomorrow. We love you." He could hear his mother's voice. It was shaky and an octave higher than normal. She must really be worried. The fact that his father said very little worried him. He knew that things must be pretty serious if his father was not speaking. Once again they both leaned down and kissed him on the forehead, then they turned and left the room.

Lucas closed his eyes for what he thought was only a minute. When he next opened his eyes the tube was gone from his throat. He could hear his parents and Dr. Lacy talking by his bedside.

Dr. Lacy looked at him and smiled. "Well that was quite some nap you took. You just slept for twelve and a half hours."

Lucas turned his head toward his parents confused. Panic filled his eyes.

Dr. Lacy spoke first. "Lucas do you know where you are?"

"In the hospital", he hoarsely whispered.

"Do you know who we are?"

"Dr. Lacy and my parents", he replied hesitantly.

"That's good Lucas. You need to listen to me. You were injured in an accident, and you're back in the states, in a hospital."

Lucas tried to remember. "An accident? I thought terrorists flew planes into the Towers. That was no accident."

Dr. Lacy and his parents looked at him confused. "Lucas, the Towers fell years ago. You enlisted in the Army. Do you remember that? You were stationed in Afghanistan. Your Humvee hit an IED."

Dr. Lacey saw the sign of remembrance in Lucas' eyes. He remembered at least part of the accident. He was not sure how much he remembered.

"I remember seeing kids running to us, and I remember hearing an explosion, then everything went black."

"Yes, that's right."

"What's wrong with me? Why can't I see?"

"Well you've got extensive injuries to your legs. They were broken in several places. They have your legs fastened back together with bars and screws. That is why you can't move them. You took some shrapnel to the face so you have several stitches, and you've sustained a slight brain injury. They're going to do some tests over the next few days to check out your vision and your hearing. As the brain swelling goes down we'll know more about the injury. You need to just rest and take it easy. It's not like you can go anywhere. I have to go back home and check on my patients, but I'll be back in a couple of days. Your parents will be staying here until they can take you home."

Lucas nodded his head. His parents sat with him and talked about what had been happening while he had been away.
They prattled on and on. When he began to tire, they kissed him and left, promising to return the next day. Lucas closed his eyes and drifted off to sleep again.

Lucas heard the children yelling to them. Like always, they wanted food or candy. With so little to eat, they constantly hounded the soldiers for food. He saw them running into the road waving their hands at the soldiers. He knew they would not have time to stop. Suddenly he heard a loud explosion. Time slowed down and everything seemed to happen in slow motion. A young boy and girl at the front of the vehicle went flying through the air. It all happened so quickly that there was no scream from them, as their limbs were ripped from their body. He knew they were dead. At the same time the children went flying, he felt the wave from the blast blow his door open and throw him through the air. He knew this was going to be bad. He didn't know if he would survive or not. His last thought before things went black was, 'please God make it quick'. Just as suddenly, Lucas found himself running down the street. He could hear the rumble behind him. He was being chased by an evil looking cloud of fire and debris and he knew the Towers were coming down. He could feel the force of the debris cloud propelling him through the air and then he hit the hard pavement. He could not get his breath.

Lucas opened his eyes. His breathing was heavy and labored. His body was covered in sweat. He tried to look around him to get his bearings. He could feel his body weighed down. Everything was black. He had just been in the Humvee and then he was running from the crumbling Towers. Where was he now? Why was he so confused? He could hear alarms going off. He heard someone walking quickly into the room and turn off the alarms.

"Well good morning Lucas. Did you have a bad dream?" The voice was soft and soothing. The hand that touched him felt cool on his warm face. He just stared blindly in the direction of the voice trying to make sense of where he was. "The doctor should be visiting you in about thirty minutes. Do you need anything?" She took a damp cloth and sponged him off.

"Water please." The nurse picked up the straw and guided it to his lips. He took a sip of water and asked, "What happened to me? Did the Towers fall on me? How long was I buried?"

"What Towers are you talking about sweetie?" she asked as she fluffed up his pillows and straightened his covers. It amazed her how much he could tangle himself up with two broken legs. He had to have been thrashing about pretty good.

"What Towers?" She could hear the agitation in his voice, "The Twin Towers."

"Lucas that happened over two years ago. You're safe in a military hospital. You just returned from Afghanistan. Now lay back, and try to relax and rest a bit. Don't worry it will all come back to you in time."

His head hurt as he tried to remember. It was frustrating not knowing what was happening and what time he was in. Everything was all mixed up. The feelings were compounded by his inability to see. He was more afraid lying in that bed than he had been when the Towers were falling. He could see what he was running from. Now he lay there unable to see anything coming or going.

Thirty minutes seemed to take forever. The doctor entered his room. "Good morning Lucas. The nurse tells me you've been having some nightmares. Well let me reassure you that those will eventually go away. She says you thought you were in the Twin Towers. Do you know what happened to you?"

"The nurse said I was in Afghanistan. I remember I was serving over there. Things keep getting all mixed up. I get bits and pieces moving around my head like a movie clip and then it switches or it is gone. I'm not always sure what is real, what is happening now or how long ago it happened."

"Why did you ask her if you had been buried under the Towers? Did you lose someone in the Towers on 9/11?"

"I knew many of the people in the Towers that were lost that day. My father's law firm was in one of the towers. My friends and I were in the Towers on 9/11. I was almost killed twice by the Towers falling. I was confused for a minute and thought that was why I was here. How long are things going to be messed up like this?"

"Once the swelling in your brain goes down completely, you should start having less confusion and memory loss. We don't know how much damage was done and how much memory loss will be permanent. Right now you seem to be making great progress. Are you able to see anything yet?"

"Things do seem a little bit lighter but that's it. Every now and then I get a flash of brighter light. Am I permanently blind? Was anyone else from my Unit killed? I remember, or at least I dreamed about some kids getting killed."

"As far as the blindness goes, we think you will regain most of your sight after the brain swelling goes down. I think there is temporary pressure on your optic nerve. I'm sorry, I don't have the information on your unit, but I can send someone in who would be able to answer those questions. They can fill you in on what happened on that mission. I believe you are well enough to hear what they say. I've scheduled a CT scan for this afternoon. We'll take another look at the brain and see how much more the swelling has gone down. We'll also take another look at your legs. I'll come back in after those tests later this afternoon and talk with you again. Right now I want you to try to eat a little to get your strength back and then just rest. Leave the worrying to us."

The doctor left the room and Lucas was left with his thoughts. Breakfast came, along with his parents. His mother began to feed him. He took one bite of the food and almost wished for his MRE's. The toaster pastry in his MRE's had more flavor than the unrecognizable mess on his tray. It was true he could not see it but he didn't recognize it either. He felt the spoon touch his lips and gently shoved his mother's hand aside.

"What is that? It tastes, no it feels slimy and kind of watery. It really has no taste. If I have to eat much more of it I'll definitely be sick. "

"It's supposed to be scrambled eggs. I can almost guarantee you that they are powdered eggs. You need to try to eat something Lucas."

His parents sounded tired and worried. He hated that he had caused them all of this pain and suffering once again. He opened his mouth and swallowed another spoonful. If it would keep them from worrying so much then he would do whatever it took to swallow the tasteless substance.

"Lucas, we were given all of your personal effects from Afghanistan. We read your letter. I know you never wanted us to have to read it. I am glad we had the opportunity to read it and tell you how proud we are of you. Your letter gave us an idea of how you felt on that day. You are our hero." Lucas smiled and once again drifted off to sleep.

After his afternoon tests, the doctor came to visit as he said he would. "I have some great news for you Lucas. The swelling is almost completely down. It seems that the shrapnel was embedded in the skull and didn't affect the brain or your optic nerve. They tell me you had the new pads under your helmet, and that absorbed most of the shock wave preventing you from having more damage. You may have some confused moments as your bruised brain tries to make new connections. You'll have minimal scarring on your face from the stitches where the shrapnel was removed. Those scars can be fixed later by a plastic surgeon. I believe your vision will slowly return. We'll take it day by day. Don't try to strain your eyes to see. The vision will come in its own time. Straining will only make it return slower. Now let's talk about your legs. They really took the brunt of the blast. Your left leg is healing nicely. You had three breaks in the tibia and one in the fibula. Your right leg is a lot worse. Your femur, tibia and fibula were shattered, as was your ankle. We've put you back together with plates and screws. We have every confidence the bones will heal nicely. You'll need quite a bit of rehab before you will be able to walk again. This is normal and time consuming. I want you to listen to the therapist because they know what is best. If you try to get ahead of yourself then you might do more damage which will need further surgery. We see you going back to a normal life in no time. Are there any questions I can answer for you?"

"I have just one. I had planned on returning from Afghanistan and continuing my education to be a PE teacher. Are my chances for that ruined now because of my injuries?"

"I see no reason why that should stop you in the least. You may have to move a little slower, but you will be able to perform all of the duties of any other PE teacher. I look forward to hearing of your progress in that area."

Lucas thanked the doctor, and laid back against the pillow. He heard his mother breathe a sign of relief.

"Mom, Dad, I want to ask you a favor."

"Whatever you want sweetheart", his mother replied as she stroked his hair.

"I want you to go home. I know you want to be here with me. I'm going to be playing the waiting game for several months. You heard the doctor. I don't mind if you call or even visit on occasion. Even though I can't see yet, I can hear the stress in your voice. That in itself, is stressing me out. I'm not trying to hurt you. I know what I have to do to get better, and I can do it better if I only have to focus on me."

"Lucas, I can't answer for your mother but I do understand. How about we stay the night and come and see you tomorrow. After that we'll go home and wait for your calls. You let us know when it is okay to visit. Is that okay with you mother?"

Mrs. James bit her lip. She didn't want to leave her son here but she knew in her heart that it was probably for the best. "Lucas if you think this will really help you with your progress then I'll agree with your dad. Please don't shut us out though. That would be too painful." She leaned forward and hugged her son. They talked for a while longer and then left promising to come back the next morning, before they left for home. They wanted their son back home with them and if this is what it would take, then they would comply.

He was ready to face the pain of rehab or whatever it would take to walk again. After all, as Trina had drilled into his and Mark's head, they were survivors and needed to act like survivors.

Lucas slowly gained his sight back. Once it had returned then the waiting for the legs was not so bad. He received letters from Afghanistan wishing him well. He loved the occasional visits from Mark and Trina. He was more than ready to get on with the rehab. His first day up was one he would not soon forget. He had to learn how to walk all over again. Sitting in the wheelchair at the end of the parallel bars he thought to himself how easy this would be. He could not have been more wrong. With two assistants to help him, one on each side, he grabbed the bars and pulled himself up. He held himself there less than five seconds and then practically fell back into the chair. It didn't matter how ready he was or how much he wanted to walk, it was evident that his legs were not yet strong enough to support him for long periods of time. He pulled himself up four more times and then called it a day. He was worn out. He was told this was how he would feel yet he had not wanted to believe it. Days went into weeks and weeks into months. Between the daily exercise, massage and manipulation of his leg muscles he began to see progress. He looked forward to the day when walking would be effortless. He knew one thing, it was prayer and his belief in not being a victim that kept him going. Whenever things got tough, and he thought of quitting, he would remember those who were laying their lives on the line every day, and push himself through the frustration and pain.

# 25 Facing the Future

It had taken Lucas six months to get to this point in his life. He felt like he finally had control of it. The Army had given him a medical discharge. He had a sixty percent disability. His legs were still messed up pretty good. He knew he would need to continue physical therapy to make them better and stronger. He was still in counseling. Most of the nightmares were gone. He struggled with the nightmare that involved the children. He knew that his experience would cause him to see children in a different light. Unlike Afghanistan, most Americans valued the lives of children. There would always be that handful of people whose minds were so warped that they did not care if they harmed a child or not. He still wanted to work with kids. He felt he was a great candidate to show them why they needed to keep their minds and bodies fit. He still had days where he was extremely depressed. Those first days when his vision began to return were tough. He was afraid of what he would see. His mind saw one thing and he didn't know if he could trust his eyes. He still grieved over the loss of his buddies and the innocent children. He was thankful to be alive, especially this day of all days. He checked his appearance in the mirror one more time before he heard a knock on the door.

"Lucas, you ready?" Mark asked with a quiver in his voice.

"On my way now." He opened the door and looked Mark up and down. "You know, we're two gorgeous looking dudes in these tuxes", he said with a chuckle. Mark slapped him on the back and they walked down the hall. He could see the pride in Mark's eyes yet recognized the nervousness in his walk. This was a big step Mark was taking. Lucas was glad to be on this journey with his friend. Mark held the door for Lucas so he could enter first. They walked to the front of the church and stood with the pastor. Lucas stood there supported by his canes. He took the opportunity to look around the church. There were his aunt and uncle, and his parents. He saw several of Marks buddies from the fire department. He looked over and saw

Trina's mother. The smile on her face gave her a heavenly glow. He knew she had lived for this day.

Suddenly the wedding march started and everyone stood and looked toward the back of the church. Trina's maid of honor and bridesmaid entered in their below the knee, lilac colored dresses. In their hands they carried a mix of lilacs and baby's breath. Trina followed the girls on her father's arm. Lucas had been right. Trina was a beautiful bride. She had chosen a strapless gown in winter white. The bodice was covered in lavender rhinestones and the skirt was covered in a beautiful, yet simple lace. She carried a simple bouquet of lavender and white baby roses, finished off with a spray of baby's breath. Her hair was pulled up. She wore a simple wreathe of baby's breath with a small piece of veiling hung from the bottom of it.

As they reached the front of the church, her father kissed her lightly on the cheek and handed her off to Mark. Lucas looked across to her maid of honor Linda and smiled. Maybe one day this would be them. They had started dating while he was in the hospital. She was a wonderful therapist, a great person to talk to, and had a deep faith. The pastor began to speak. They all turned and faced him, and their futures.

# Author's Note

The people depicted in this story are fictional; however, I based the events on eyewitness accounts on that terrible day. This story came about because I was in a classroom on that morning in Bradenton, Florida when one of my students came charging down the hallway screaming about a plane flying into the Twin Towers. She begged me to turn on the television. As we stood watching the news, we watched live as the second plane flew into the second Tower. Our school had us leave the televisions on all day. I spent most of the day trying to reassure my students that everything would be okay, and that they would be safe. I didn't feel that way. My husband's sister lived a short distance from the Pentagon and said the explosion was so violent that her dishes were rattled out of their cabinets. We knew many who had friends that worked in the Pentagon or had family in New York. That evening we received a call from my youngest sister. Her former roommate worked in one of the Towers. It was several months before her family had her declared legally dead. Her body was one of many, never recovered.

The whole country was touched that day. Ten months later, in July, my husband, daughter and I arrived in New York City for a National Dance competition. We toured ground zero and I cried. My husband and I went back and toured ground zero again without our daughter. We saw such a sad and frightening sight. Yet, while we were there I felt like I was in the safest place on earth. I could feel the friendliness of the city. We saw people reaching out to each other. Total strangers talked to us about their city and places we would enjoy. So many lives were lost that day yet we saw the true spirit of America there, in all of the faces we saw. This is a day we will remember forever because it was a day we all became survivors. America did not become a victim. We picked up the pieces and moved on.

This book is dedicated to everyone who lost their life, or a loved one on that day.

Made in the USA
Coppell, TX
24 March 2022